FALLING THROUGH THE CRACKS

by Fritzie Rogers

Falling Through the Cracks

by Fritzie Rogers

New Victoria Publishers

Published by New Victoria Publishers Inc. P.O. Box 27 Norwich, Vermont 05055

Illustrations and cover design by Ginger Brown
Printed on recycled paper
ISBN 0-934678-29-4

Library of Congress Cataloging-in-Publication Data

Rogers, Fritzie, 1927-
    Falling through the cracks : a novel / by Fritzie Rogers
        p.   cm.
     ISBN 0-934678-29-4
     I. Title.
     PS3568.0435F3   1991
     813' .54- -dc-20   91-43724
                                          CIP

Prologue

The years 1969 to 1976 were the shank of the Nixon Recession, but unless her (or his) life got wrecked, your average American had never heard of the Nixon Recession, nor had your average California hard-worker considered the possibility of being unemployed and penniless, until it happened. Yet there they were, 100,000 high-tech employees in the Unemployment lines after the Apollo space program collapsed and defense orders dwindled in hopeful anticipation of a quick victory in the war in Vietnam.

It happened so quickly. You were out of work. Then one day you faced it—this time there was to be no job for you for some time to come, your old friends thought you were low life, your family was treating you like a poor relation.

That day you moved to Los Angeles' only beach, Venice, *"seeking out the poorer quarters where the ragged people go,"* as Paul Simon put it. There you took care of someone else if you couldn't take care of yourself. In that way everyone survived until tomorrow.

As usual in bad times as well as good, Venice was packed with gays and lesbians, sleeping anywhere and doing everything everywhere. No one could afford Berkeley, San Francisco's Castro, Santa Monica or West Hollywood since urban gentrification had begun already. Unless you were a devout Nixon Republican, Laguna Beach was out of the question. All that was left were East Los Angeles and Venice.

Why Venice? Because it's always Venice. Venice was there for the Bohemians, for the Lost Generation, for the Beatniks and for the Flower Children of the 1960's. It was there for us in the Nixon Recession, and it will be there for you when your life goes rotten, as it could some day.

If Venice is a town for throw-away people, it may be because Venice itself is a throw-away town. Earlier this century an energetic real estate developer built the town to mimic Venice, Italy, with a romantic atmosphere created by a network of canals. These prospects for enormous profit paled when oil was discovered.

Immediately the land and mineral rights were sold to the drilling companies who let the town go to seed. Most of the canals were filled with dirt and converted to roads, except for a small community, called The Canals, which maintains a heady, romantic ambiance of brackish water, foot-bridges, old houses and a fleet of wild water-fowl.

If you hurry you may have a chance to walk through The Canals in the evening and believe, as thousands before you, that the world is truly beautiful. But hurry. The Canals will soon be gobbled up by the greed and opulence of the Marina del Rey.

Here, then, are pieces of our lives from a time when that was all there was.

Chapter 1

Stinson Beach, near San Francisco.

The sound of sneakers in the gravel roused Sue before the sun was up. She pushed back the knit cap and poked her round face out of her sleeping bag. As she rubbed the dust from her blue eyes and stared out the rear window of her hearse, she saw Kimmey running in place behind the chrome and black left fin. As chilly as it was in the May morning, Kim's long tan limbs were beginning to shine from perspiration; a streak of sweat showed down the back of her tank top, and her otherwise straight brown hair was curling around her headband.

"I've got it!" shouted Kim.

"So come in already!" Sue opened the double doors on the left, the corpse doors, for Kimmey who was her usual morning guest. Kimmey climbed in and flopped across to the jump seat in the 'live' entry. "Start up the heater and put on a tape before you get settled," muttered Sue through a bad case of smoker's hack.

With the experienced air of a privileged guest, Kim leaned through the sliding glass window into the driver's cab and turned the key to ignite the engine and the heater. After a minimal search she found the Crosby, Stills, Nash and Young and pushed it into the slot. By the time she was again installed in the jump seat, the Sterno can was blistering water in the small aluminum pan, and Sue was spooning instant coffee into the plastic cups, and asking, "You've got what, besides infectious hepatitis?"

"The name for your hearse, that's what I've got."

Sue took a swig of the hot liquid. "I'm ready."

1

"Its name is William Randolph."

"Why didn't I think of that?"

"As a reward can you take me in to San Raphael this p.m., for more gamma globulin?"

Sue chuckled into her coffee cup. "Have you been up all night working out this ploy to get to town?" Kim smiled boldly and shifted on the jump-seat, self-consciously awaiting Sue's answer. "As it happens," Sue continued, "today is the day the San Raphael Unemployment tells me how much the State of Illinois is going to pay me."

"Perfect. You can drop me at the Free Clinic, and I can walk to Unemployment afterwards. Now let's go back to my—excuse me, Patty's—house first. We haven't had a sauna and shower for days."

"I thought you'd never ask!" While they finished their coffee Sue rolled up the sleeping bag and rummaged in the foot locker for a towel and clean clothes. The very thought of being completely clean again made her itch even more than she usually did, waking up in yesterday's clothes. A cigarette helped, the first of the day, hand-rolled the night before from Bugler tobacco and conveniently placed on the dashboard above the lighter. Nicotine on top of the caffeine put the white back in her corneas but had no appreciable effect on the toothache that had taken up residence in an upper molar next to her front bridgework.

At the house on top of the hill the sun was up already. Sue set out her clean clothes to warm on the wooden deck, shed her dirty jeans and shirt into a pile beside them. For a few minutes she warmed her back before dashing under the house and into the sauna. Kim had already stoked the fire in the small pot-bellied stove. The two women set themselves on the pine bench while the air in the tiny, tight room turned woody and then piping hot.

When they were sure they couldn't stand the heat any more, they threw open the door, slammed it shut behind them, and hurried the few steps to the slatted open deck nearby. Kimmey pulled the chain, and the overhead shower doused them with blue-cold water pumped from the creek beside them. Still numb, they baked again and drenched again, until their skins were

2

pink and cold and clean.

Sue finished off with a shampoo. By the time she was ready to dry her mouse-brown hair in the sun, Kim was sound asleep. Two kittens, Narcissus and Goldman, played 'hunting' in her crotch and over her stomach. Another hectic day at Stinson Beach was under way. It was time for a little nap.

Some time later the smell of chicken noodle soup jump-started Sue into late-morning consciousness. With the sun on their backs, she and Kim blew and slurped until energy infused their limbs.

"I wish," Kim mused, "Patty would get vegetable beef soup for a change."

Sue laughed. "What you've got, besides hepatitis, is a dependency problem."

"What's a...dependency problem?"

"Actually, it's more like a question, in your case, who's going to buy the vegetable beef soup?"

"You suggest a novel if revolting possibility."

Before they could think of dressing, there came a noisy splashing and a soggy racket from the shower deck around the corner. Four dripping, naked and suntanned young women chased each other up the wooden steps, stopping abruptly at the bench where Kim and Sue lay digesting in the sunshine.

"Kimmers!" exclaimed the biggest one, Nola, six feet of suntanned surfer with a big white smile, bright blue eyes, and more than her fair share of blonde hair.

"Nola, you old whore! What lured you to Stinson?" asked Kim.

"Nola was developing an attitude in Frisco," came another voice, splattering words like machine-gun bullets. "So we came out here to play, where I can keep an eye on her." The origin of this possessive invective was Thea. She had an explosive smile to match her voice, a mop of curly hair in a permanent tangle, and a pound of silver chains and pendants on her neck.

"Holy Toledo! Who's this!" said Nola, gaze fixed on Sue, who had never believed her own lazing sunburned nakedness to be any more than serviceable.

"Like I said, an attitude," came as machine-gun bullets from

3

Thea.

"Everybody!" inserted Kim. "This here is my pal Sue, better known as Sleepy. Sleepy, standing before you are four residents of that notorious suburb of L.A., the city of Venice. Your admirer is Nola, and the one giving her the knee is her better half, Thea."

With considerable relief Sue noted that Thea was smiling and hoped her anger was reserved for Nola.

"...And over there we have Evelyn the all-American girl...," Kim continued, indicating a sturdy young woman whose shining brown hair was braided down to her waist, with loose bangs at her forehead.

"...And Flor." She pointed her eyes at an earthy and inviting chicana with a white towel across her shoulders. Kim and Flor stood there, each wilting at the sight of the other, ready to melt together like two comic-book characters and float between the floorboards.

Evelyn retrieved Flor's attention with a possessive arm around her waist, and broke the sensual current between Kim and Flor with some quick preventive conversation. "We missed seeing you at Maude's Bar last night, Kim, so we came out here for a while before heading home to Venice."

"Oh, uh, yeah," said Kim. She backed away flustered by Evelyn's barely veiled hostility. "Stick around as long as you want, guys; but me and Sue have a couple of vital errands in San Raphael. Just pull the door shut when you leave." While they could still maintain their decisiveness, Kim and Sue put on their stiff-clean jeans, tucked in their Hawaiian print shirts, and ran for the hearse.

When they were safely on the road Kim said, "Nola was really coming on to you!"

"I wish it were otherwise," Sue replied, mindful of the hot spots under her eyes and in other more interesting places. "Thea scares the liver out of me."

"Don't let Thea throw you. You'll see what a pussy cat she is."

Sue's curiosity got the best of her at last. "I've never seen you in love before. What's with you and Flor?"

Kim shifted around in the passenger's seat. "I guess it's pretty obvious. It happens just like that every time we see each other. I swear, we've never been together. I don't think we've even been in the same room alone. Talk about fear! Evelyn is to be worried about! I think you and I got out of the house just in time to prevent World War Three."

"I always thought you and Patty were a big item," said Sue.

"No big item ever prevented me from falling in love."

"We're coming into Mill Valley. Time to zip up your fly."

"Flor," mused Kim. "An easy way to mess up a clean pair of jeans. Speaking of compulsions, how are you making out with Yaz?"

"Rotten. Can't get to first base. She wouldn't even dance with me at Maude's Bar last Saturday. Always What's His Face hanging around her cabin door. I tell you, Kim, these bisexual women drive me up a tree."

"I really don't think you should give up. I know for a personal fact she can be had, and I also know she likes you."

"Maybe so. But I doubt my self-image can stand rejection long enough to find out. Personally, I think she's got someone else on her mind. But Yaz sure sticks in my mind. What makes Yaz so damned attractive anyway?"

"It's no secret," Kim confessed. "I myself could go for a round or two with Yaz. Yazmina has that soft look, like Flor, only with Yaz it comes from being half Danish and half Persian. And she's a nurse. Nursing is so physical."

Sue stopped the hearse on the street in front of an office. "Here's your gamma globulin."

Sue shuffled out of Unemployment with her hands shoved into her pockets, opened the front door of the hearse and slid in. "Sons of bitches," she said softly, not above a vicious whisper, but the anger resounded all the way to Illinois and back. Kim started in her sleep, even behind the sliding glass which she opened in a hurry for the verdict.

"What did they say?"

"How am I going to live on forty dollars a week?" She blinked at the tears as they ran rivulets from her cheeks to her chops.

"Holy cow, Sue! That's a rough go!"

"For twenty-one years I worked in the state of California,

5

paying their fucking income tax, workman's compensation, gas tax, property tax, sales tax, and unemployment insurance. Then I get unemployed, go to work in Illinois for six months until the company folds. Here I am, back in California, out of a job again, and California acts as if it never heard of me! Illinois pays forty dollars a week and that's all I can get." By the time this oration was over, Sue's face, screwed up into an angry knot, was covered by her hands.

After Sue cried for several more minutes, with Kim hugging, she was ready for logic again. "What am I going to do? Find another job? Not any time soon. That silly job in Illinois was my first work in over a year, and I don't hear any offers. By the time they'll want a computer programmer again I'll have been unemployed so long my career will be in the toilet."

"At least you have William Randolph," Kim reminded her. "That's more than I've got."

"Who's...? Oh yeah! The hearse!" Sue laughed and then assumed yoga position in the driver's seat. "You know, that's a really great name. It resolves his personality conflict. I always thought he was either a hearse or an ambulance. Now he can be a closet limousine with the kind of class he richly deserves." Sue started the big engine and they headed off toward Stinson for lack of a better place to go. "William Randolph is trustworthy, like a Boy Scout. With William Randolph I always have a place to sleep with my head off the pavement." She shook her head in despair. "But the nights get so cold around here. I need a real home."

"If I were you," ventured Kim, "I'd go down to Venice for a while. It's a lot warmer than the Bay area, and prices are a whole lot lower. Your forty bucks might last a week. Besides, there's more action, if you know what I mean, and want to know the honest truth."

"Action. The very sound of the word pushes my buttons. So far I'm getting nowhere with Yazmina. Hmm. It couldn't hurt to drive down and have a look around. Why don't you declare yourself a vacation from the back-breaking rush around Stinson, and come along? You can get more gamma globulin at a Free Clinic, down there as easily as up here."

6

"A few days in the rays couldn't hurt," Kim said enthusiastically. "Heh heh. Patty's Frisco finks haven't been out to Stinson recently. So the Witch doesn't know I'm clean again and ready to trot." Kim's mood clouded again. "Eventually she'll show up in that black Ferrari. We'll shoot up until I'm strung out, and she'll dump me out here at Stinson again."

"So you might as well play in Venice for a change. We can share the gas, and sleep in the hearse."

"I've got plenty of good Venice connections; we can probably sleep inside."

Sue saw her prospects brighten. "I'd sure like to *connect* with a particular Venice *connection* we left in the sun on your back deck."

"I'll bet Danny Mae has room at Highland House over on Linnie Canal. How about leaving tomorrow morning?"

"Why not?"

In another half hour William Randolph slushed his Cadillac self around the last mountain curve and galumphed along the stretch, down and down toward the silvered Drake's Bay. As they approached "Stinson Beach Centro," Kim said, "There's Nancy's VW, stopped at Yaz's Peachbottom Flats. Maybe she would feed Narcissus and Goldman while I'm gone for a week."

They parked in front of the Sand Dollar Bar and went across the road to where Yaz, in her usual semi to maximum nudity, was hosing down the deck at Peachbottom: Local dyke residence and half-way house for recovery from overdose on civilization.

"Hey Nan-cy!" hollered Kim as she flung open the gate and ran indoors looking for her.

"We're going down to El Lay in the morning," Sue announced to anyone who cared to hear her.

"Far-fucking-out!" said Yaz from the water-works. "In that case you had better settle over on the porch and let me do your cards. I must say, your aura looks good today."

"It must be the sauna this morning," said Sue as she set herself on the warm wooden step. She really didn't believe any of this mysticism, but she appreciated Yaz's concern for her immediate future. Besides, ever since Yaz's brain concussion in a car wreck, her tarots were really colorful.

Yaz shuffled the cards, let Sue cut them, and then laid them out. "You're Scorpio, as I recall. Aha! Your Cups are running over. Buckets of money! Everywhere I look, buckets of money! And here's you and Death and a trip, but it's not bad news. How weird! That's got to be you in the hearse going to Los Angeles. But here's something strange, for a Scorpio: All around you I see love, but not involving you. This isn't just a trip, is it. You're actually moving to Los Angeles? I don't know whether to advise this move or not."

There was a puzzled sadness in those black Persian eyes that made Sue wonder if maybe she'd be missed. Maybe she should put the trip off for a while. Recalling something her lesbian great-aunt used to say about "throwing good money after bad," Sue let her common sense take over and replied, "Under my present circumstances, I can hardly refuse your promise of money. Love can wait for next year. It looks like a good omen to me."

Meanwhile Nancy poured vodka-clamato juice. She and Kim began negotiating cat diets and venues. "Do you think," Nancy asked, "that Narcissus and Goldman can share with Handsome Prince? He gets older and crabbier every day. Well, he's too slow to hurt them any, and they can just hide under something lower than he is fat."

Kim nodded. "I think they'd enjoy a little vacation. The kids travel pretty well. I had them with me down here yesterday, and they stayed inside most of the time, except for crapping time, and they found the cat door all by themselves."

"Narcissus and Goldman couldn't be better guests," Yaz assured everyone.

"Who's Handsome Prince?" Sue inquired, two paragraphs behind everyone else and getting groggy.

"Handsome Prince? Well," Nancy began, "for years I had a scruffy old yellow tom cat named Charlie; until one day someone ran over him with a truck outside of Ed's Superette Number One. I'll tell you, I was in deep mourning, and then one noon I heard someone at the door and there stood this young tom looking exactly like Charlie but as good as new. He winked at me, wrapped his fat tail around my leg and said, 'My name is Hand-

8

some Prince and I am Charlie returned. I have come to live with you.' And that was that."

Yaz, who was still all but naked, wet from the hose and constitutionally temperature-sensitive, suggested they move the party indoors. Then she crawled into bed while she still could find it.

"Yaz smoothed out a patch of bedclothes just big enough for Sue to sprawl in, which she did.

In a little while Kim went up on the roof and adjusted the TV antenna. They finished the evening watching re-runs of horror movies on the Fright Night TV show. Who could ask for a nicer farewell?

Chapter 2

Kim loaded Sue into the hearse and took her home for the night. Wrapped up in blankets, Sue shared the couch with Narcissus and Goldman, secured against the cold ocean air and the inevitability of bronchitis. It was well past nine AM by the time she stirred, with the stereophonic whirring of a hungry kitten in each ear.

Kim, more accustomed than Sue to waking up without the sun in her eyes, had been up long enough to make a thermos of coffee for the trip, and two cups to wake up with. She put the cups on the raw wooden antique orange crate near Sue's nose and removed the kittens to their breakfast in the kitchen. She lit two Pall Malls off the pilot light and took up Yogi position by the couch.

"I thought you quit smoking," Sue chided, accepting a lit cigarette with one eye open. "Your guru would be disgusted."

"My guru," Kim retorted between drags, "is a junkie."

"Do you think we could ever quit smoking?" Sue wondered to the air.

"All I know is, I go cold turkey on cocaine and/or heroin every so often, but it's no use trying to give up tobacco. Here, I've been to Superette's for doughnuts. And then you can comb and fix up in the back of William Randolph, while I drive us over to Nancy's and leave the kittens in bed with her."

By the time they waved bye-bye to Stinson and passed by Mount Tamalpais, Sue had tucked her dirty shirt into the laundry bag, and got a fresh one from the foot-locker. Her UCLA sweatshirt she left on the jump seat, just in case of a chill in the Bay fog. Kim flung open the window between them. "I haven't

10

been to Mount Tam since the End of the World party. Remember that one?"

"That was before my time."

"Yeah. Sometimes I forget you're a tourist. Anyway, when I got home I found a note from Patty on the door: *Sorry I have to miss the End of the World. See you afterwards at the Blue Whale Bar.* How much gas do you suppose is in this tank? We're driving on E already."

"In this case, E stands for Enough. We can get to Oakland if we have to," said Sue. "But let's fill up at the cheapie station where US 101 comes out of Golden Gate Park." She widened the gap in the partitioning glass, and dove into the front seat. The '58 Caddy hearse was wide enough for about anything.

It was Kim's turn to think ahead. "It's not too early for a pit stop at Maude's. Rickey will cash a few of my traveler's checks, and we can put in some cold ones for the road."

"I wonder if Rickey is speaking to me anymore," Sue said.

"Why in hell not?"

"Last Saturday, after I gave up on Yaz, I crashed out with my face on the bar. Somehow Rickey resented having to ask those two new lesbian cops to carry me, unconscious, into the back room. I wouldn't blame her if she's a little testy."

"At least she kept you out of jail. Rickey's like that. Doesn't she know about your narcolepsy?" asked Kim.

"No. I slunk out the back way as soon as I woke up."

"Just leave it to the old Kim. Maybe...Maybe you had better let me drive the whole way to Venice."

"There's really nothing to worry about. I get symptoms before I get sleepy, so I just pull over and get a few z's. That would be a good time for you to take over the wheel for a while. If you ever feel unsafe, say so. I'm not so proud or vain that I like to push myself close to the ultimate limits of my abilities."

"I've gotta say, I've had the sweats a time or two with you at the wheel. I won't shine it on from now on. I'll bet this crashing thing gives you plenty of trouble...socially, I mean."

Sue began to giggle. "I remember the first time it happened in public. I was at a Chinese restaurant in West Covina, with my husband and my lover."

11

"These were two separate people?" Kim inquired with both eyebrows raised.

"Yep, and two separate sexes. You would think the situation would preclude crashing, but that's not the way narcolepsy works. The more excited I am, the faster I fall asleep. I woke up with my face in the chicken chow yuk."

Kim was screaming with laughter. "I hope you kept the rice out of your nose and didn't talk in your sleep. Has it ever happened when you?...you know what I mean."

"You have stumbled onto the great secret to my unpopularity. So far, only Marlene has handled it gracefully. Marlene was an insomniac, so she didn't think I was more than average disappoiting."

Rickey hadn't yet unlocked the door to Maude's Bar when Sue pulled the hearse into the bus stop at the corner in San Francisco. "You can't park here," said Kim. "Not in the daytime. They'll tow you away and impound you unless it's after sundown."

"Thanks, pal," said Sue. "If they do it to anyone, they'll do it to me, in this weird wagon we're driving. It's a good thing I'm not paranoid."

"Denial will get you nowhere. Hey! Back around the corner and head back toward Maude's. I see two cars leaving at the same time, right in front of the place!"

Back and forth, this way and that. Finally William Randolph was safe in two adjacent parking spaces. Sue sighed, pulled out the key and commented, "Which all goes to prove Bob and Ray's rule, The Artie Skirmirhorn Principle: Wherever you're going, there's a place waiting for you to park right in front."

By that time Maude's door was swung wide outward and a bar stool set in front to keep it open and tether it to the wall. With the sun at ten o'clock AM, you could see better inside than at midnight with all the lights ablaze.

"Good morning, ladies," said Rickey as she set out a beer for Kim and a tall glass of orange juice for Sue.

"Good morning, teacher," came an expansive voice from over their left shoulders as four visions in blue denim moved in and

12

settled at the east end of the bar.

Kim whispered, "We'd better make a move on the toilets before this tribe remembers their bladders."

"I'll be hiding in the men's crapper. "Nothing in the world is cleaner or quieter than the men's room in a lesbian bar. As Sue sat there in solitary comfort she counted up everyone of her immediate acquaintance who had problems too large or too painful to discuss. All in all, she preferred her own troubles, except for a blinding toothache which by now had become permanent.

While she was examining the tooth with her tongue, something heavy fell out of it and clanked along the lower molars. It didn't take a genius to recognize it as a gold inlay with an infusion of blackened tooth enamel. It wasn't hard to tell a candidate for a root canal. Ten years ago it would have cost a hundred dollars; at present inflated costs and her deflated income...never mind ruining an otherwise pleasant day.

"Shit!" said Kimmey when she got the news. "With your luck the past week, be glad you're not straight. You'd turn up pregnant."

One of the denim quartet slipped up onto the stool next to Sue. "If you two are going through Oakland, how about a lift?"

"Sure, if you don't mind getting off on the highway."

Rickey put a six-pack in a bag for Kim, and pressed a roll of mini-benny cross-tops into Sue's palm. "Here's a present from the house to you. San Francisco Bart laid these on me last week. I never use them, but according to Kim it seems maybe you could use something to help you to stay awake. I believe I greatly misjudged your character, honey. From now on we'll take better care of you in here."

"I was just about to thank you for keeping me out of jail!"

It was eleven o'clock when the troupe departed, Kimmey at the wheel and the denim dyke in the back, mortally shocked when she discovered where she was. "Jesus! Doesn't this yacht ever give you the creeps?"

Sue was used to slander. "Prepare for the ultimate in comfort. You'll be asleep before we leave the Haight, so tell us now where we should let you off."

Several miles after their passenger stepped down in Oakland Sue shouted, "Damn! The bitch stole my UCLA sweatshirt!"

Kim assumed a philosophical air. "If you do some people the slightest favor, they really make you pay for it. I think we left town just in time. Next stop is for gas in Cunnilingus."

"Coalinga, Kimmey, Coalinga!"

Sue Awake

Chapter 3

The white-on-blue sign next to the Interstate exit said,
   COALINGA Gas Food Lodging
"I'll bet we can make it to the next stop," said the ever-optimistic Kimmey from the driver's seat.

"Don't kid yourself, kid. When a sign on Interstate 5 says gas, you gotta get it. If we don't get off at Coalinga, you can plan on walking back to it." Sue could only hope she got through to Kim, who tended to take unreasonable if optimistic chances.

Kim took the exit, and they filled up William Randolph's huge tanks and the beverage cooler. "I didn't mean to scare you back there," Kimmey confessed. "Dry on this road is the last thing I want to be. Have you ever seen a highway so long and hot and dreary and scary?"

Sue opened a beer for Kim and a Coke for herself. "The trip used to be fun, on Highway 99 with all the juice stands and funny towns. If they would fix up old 99 I would use it today." After a steamy drive past irrigated cotton fields they were again on the desert floor and on the break-neck climb up the Grapevine. "At least they haven't mucked around with the Grapevine. Racing up this long old grade is still a thrill."

There is something about speeding on the freeways that makes you feel like you belong in the fast lane. There is something about the smell of Southern California smog. No matter how long you've been gone, whether or not you have ever lived there, you know when you're home. Get one whiff, and it's got you by the tits forever. And so it was that when her long black 'meat wagon' pushed its nose over the last rise of the Grapevine, two hearts skipped a beat.

Way off in the far distance the sun was setting over the Pacific Ocean and turning the sky to purple over the San Fernando Valley. From behind came a bright pink light, the unseen sunset reflecting off the gray San Gabriel Mountains. Ahead, at ground level, three double strands of red lights wound around but always forward and downward. It was rush hour on the Four Oh Five Freeway.

For thirty minutes they rolled southward and downward at sixty-five miles per hour past Magic Mountain and the new and gleaming high-rise office buildings and condos of Van Nuys and Glendale. Traffic thickened, finally congealing to a molasses crawl until they reached the top of Sepulveda Pass through the Santa Monica Mountains. Then the speed of traffic doubled again while the density of vehicles remained the same, a ridiculous paradox amenable to Kim's raceway personality.

Off to the left some distance eastward were the lights of Century City. It looked for all the world like The Emerald City of Oz with the Yellow Brick Road of the Santa Monica Freeway through the jeweled carpet of city lights. L.A. had been scrubbed and polished for their homecoming.

Traffic loosened up as they got closer to Culver City, finally becoming navigable when they came to the Marina Freeway (also known as the Richard M. Nixon Freeway, which prophetically went nowhere). At its end was Lincoln Boulevard, which passed the gleam of Marina del Rey. A few blocks later they turned onto Venice Boulevard, pot-holed and wash-boarded but nevertheless the gateway to Venice West.

Finally, a hard left at the grocery led them across two bridges to the hush of The Canals. With no trouble they found a place to put William Randolph by a park. From nowhere a tall dog arrived to baptize the right rear fender.

When their hair was combed and shirts tucked in, Kim and Sue opened the doors and stepped out into Never-Never Land. By flashlight they walked a block down Linnie quay, listening to the high snap of the bongo drums and watching a fleet of ducks cruise by on the canal.

At last Kim stopped at a picket fence and caught a handwritten sign in the flashlight beam: *Don't Trample The Duck-*

lings. The two women stepped over the fence and high grass and found themselves at Highland House. In the flower garden beside the gate was a row of disembodied plastic dolls' hands placed in the soil as if they grew there like plants. These and a similar crop of smiling faces were a sure sign that Danny Mae lived there.

Kim knocked at the door, and someone inside turned down the television. "Kimmey!" came a raspy, yet musical woman's voice from somewhere inside. The door swung open and there stood Danny, sturdy and tanned, all tits and muscles in a white T-shirt, blonde hair in studied disarray. Her bright blue eyes behind steel-rimmed glasses were the color of Santa Monica Bay, and her smile was as broad and sunny as Venice Beach.

"Hey Danny! I brought you a recruit!" By then Kim and Danny were climbing all over each other and everyone else was shouting except Sue who stood in the doorway with one hand in the other, not knowing what to do. Finally everyone resumed whatever they were doing, in this case a new ki of grass.

Danny stretched her bluejeans into Yoga position, hiked her white T-shirt out in back and pounded a piece of the floor next to her, and said to Sue, "Come over and sit down. What brings you to town?"

"In San Francisco I can't live on forty a week from Unemployment, and I thought it might be possible down here. I've lived in Southern California most of my adult life, anyway, so it's like coming home."

"Forty a week? You're one of the rich ones! Most Unemployment Insurance has run out already, although we're hoping Congress will give us an extension. We all hang together around here so we won't hang separately. Where are you staying?"

"Kim and I came down in my hearse...."

"A hearse?"

"Goes by the name of William Randolph, when it goes."

"Well, all right! What do you do for a living, ordinarily, I mean?"

"Up until a year ago I was a computer programmer in aerospace."

"Man!" exclaimed Danny. "If there's no work for you, what

hope is there for the rest of us? Wow! Well, any friend of Kim's is a friend of mine. We're packed solid when it comes time to sleep, so maybe you and Kim could spend one more night in Wiliam Randolph while I think about where to put you on a more permanent basis. Evelyn will show you around this zoo."

At that moment Evelyn appeared, sleepy and disoriented, from somewhere behind the piano.

"Evelyn!" exclaimed Sue. "How did you guys get down here from Stinson so fast?"

"We had return tickets on the Twenty-Dollar Red-eye flight."

"I hardly recognized you dressed," quipped Sue.

"Around Venice, nude and dressed have a great deal in common," Evelyn responded. Their tour started with the shower. "This holds two comfortably, but can't compare with the sauna in Stinson."

Evelyn's space was behind the upright piano whose raw back was mitigated by an Indian batik. The opposing wall was strewn with posters and other offerings from the Hari Krishnas, various astrologers, L. Ron Hubbard, and a home-grown flier for something going on at the Venice Beach Pavilion. A line of nails received a collection of inspired hats. A narrow path allowed access to the sleeping-sitting space, a sleeping bag unfurled upon a slack air mattress. Back of that, against the remaining wall, was a steel foot locker topped with two fat candles, a box of incense, and an ash tray and matches. A bunch of keys on a beaded fob lay carelessly near the edge.

Similar spaces, individually unique but indistinguishable, accommodated uncounted inhabitants behind doors, at the ends of halls, in the pantry, the service porch and gardener's shed out back. Everywhere there was an amazing definition of territory and preservation of privacy.

By the time the tour was finished, Sue was properly proud to have been admitted to this haphazard but classy bunch. Nevertheless, she was relieved to have William Randolph to curl up in and forty dollars a week to subsist on. Somehow her poverty in San Francisco had turned to riches in Venice. Venice was magic.

Chapter 4

The next morning came as early as any other. What was missing was Kim, whose bed roll was still cold and stashed behind the jump seat. She must have gotten lucky some place. Although it was only slightly past dawn, Sue decided to see what Highland House was like in the mornings. The front door opened to her easy push, and her nose was regaled by the smell of fresh coffee. In charge at the stove was a black male in cutoff jeans, bare feet, and a fiercely cultivated Afro.

Sue tried her voice. "Good morning. I'm Sue."

"Try a shot of this," he said, handing over a pottery cup full of coffee. "You're the new one from up north. I'm Charles. Let's sit outside so we don't disturb the local zombies. They won't be moving until about ten."

As they sat on the stoop, elbows on knees, sipping coffee, the postman loped over the bridge and down the quay toward them on his way to work. He looked like any other postman except that he wore rubber sandals, blue wool trousers cut off above the knees, his shirt open to the navel with no tie, and his hair was long to match his beard. When he saw Charles and Sue, he stopped in his tracks. "How come you two are up so early?"

"Oh," Charles answered casually, "we went to college." The postman laughed, threw up his hands and went bobbing down the quay.

"Sue."Charles pondered. "That must be short for Susan?"

"No. It's spelled *Sioux....*"

Charles exploded with laughter. "As in Ogalala Sioux?"

"Ultimately, I suppose," said Sue, stifling the giggles. "On my birth certificate my name is Sioux Falls. It was Mother's idea.

19

Dad wanted Boisie."

"Are your folks clinically sane?"

"Sure. Just slightly sadistic."

When the coffee had done its work, it was time for action. "It must be seven o'clock," Charles observed. "If we each have half a dollar, we can go to the The Germans' for breakfast."

Sue scratched around in her jeans for the part of her wealth not stashed in her money belt. "Two bucks!" Charles exclaimed enthusiastically. He had something over a dollar, so off they went across two bridges and down the Venice Boulevard median to the beach.

The last structure on Venice Beach, just before it becomes Marina del Rey, was a squat frame building with a beer bar at one end and a small, unmarked restaurant on the other. The sign in the window said: *Open seven AM, Closed ten-thirty AM,* obviously dedicated to local trade only. All the doors and windows were opened wide to expel the rich smells that attracted customers from all over town.

"This is one of only three places in the world where I ever stand in line," said Charles. The line extended half a block from the restaurant and wasn't so much a line as a social function all by itself. After Sue met everyone in line, and the past night's comings and goings were sorted out, half an hour was gone.

At last Sue and Charles found places to sit, miraculously next to one another at the L-shaped counter with an assortment of movable stools. Elsa, an attractive blonde woman of about twenty-five, took their orders, and they had a few minutes to watch the action.

Back of the counter were two belching stoves, one reserved for bacon, sausages, and fried potatoes; the other reserved for eggs, French toast and pancakes. The action behind the counter was directed and choreographed by Mama, a fifty-ish widowed West German immigrant who both cooked at one of the stoves and directed her three grown children. "John, I'm running out of batter over here and Pete needs some sausage. Elsa," Mama whispered, "James is here. I know his Disability check isn't here yet, so give him a blank ticket." As far as anyone could remember, no one went away hungry.

Almost as soon as their orders were in the food was in front of them. Sue and Charles ate quickly and took their coffee with them out to a bench by Ocean Front Walk. While they relaxed and digested a while, the Venice locals streamed in and out.

"Come on," said Charles, "I'll take you on a walking tour of the beach before we go home."

After returning the coffee cups to the Germans' they walked northward past the beer bar, several boarded-up retail shops and Mary's Burgers, alive but asleep until noon. Next was the kids playground and the Parks and Recreation office. "The City gives out free lunches here, to anyone who shows up. Pretty good, too. Always a carton of milk, some kind of meat sandwich with lettuce and tomato, and fruit, usually an orange. I know run-aways and old people who would die without the lunch program."

A rasping drunken voice came at them from a bench between the muscle builders' club and the senior citizens' clubhouse. "Hey, Charles! Found a nice piece of ass so early in the day?"

"No, Auraville. Sue here is a new recruit at Highland House."

Shaking his head in disbelief Auraville said, "A terrible waste of talent."

Turning to Charles, Sue asked, "What in the world is a handsome heterosexual dude like you doing, living in Highland House with all those lesbians? There can't be much sexual gratification."

Charles' brown face flushed in spite of himself. "Well, in the first place I'm not as hetero as I look. For another thing, you'd be amazed how many have a heterosexual side to them. If nothing else, I'm a patient man."

"How in hell did you find Highland House?"

"In a way, I was there first. Last summer, when Danny found me, I was living on the beach and hustling under the pier at Pacific Ocean Park."

"I thought that POP closed years ago," Sue said.

"Officially it did, but it's still a playground, of sorts. If you do nothing else this morning, you gotta see POP. But there's a lot more between here and there."

Charles walked them another block and stopped in the mid-

21

dle of the street at Windward, the official entry to Venice Beach. The scene was as dismal as the face of the moon. "Is everything boarded up around here?" asked Sue. "Doesn't anything work?"

"My dear, you are standing at the cultural center of Venice Beach. Roll the drums, bang the cymbals. Over there is a liquor store catering to morning drunks, a pawn shop, and across the street there's a one-room department store always having a sale and going out of business." Charles turned slowly westward and pointed a long, bony finger. "And there is the Venice Pavilion," he said.

"Pavilion?" said Sue. "I don't see any pavilion."

"Well, do you see the wall?"

"What wall?"

"Try 'grass,' in front of the wall."

"Ah!" said Sue. "Like any environment, you have to learn to see stuff in it. It's a long wall, the color of sand. No wonder I couldn't see it. I still can't see the pavilion."

Charles laughed. "BEHIND the wall. The pavilion has been boarded up until a few weeks ago. The City is letting us put on a home-grown, free rock opera. It's doing really well."

Farther on down Ocean Front Walk all of the stores were boarded except the Lafayette Restaurant with inside murals of Paris amid a strong odor of sausages. "We all come here for breakfast on Mondays when the Germans' is closed, or on any day we get up too late for the Germans' short open hours. They have real booths to sit in."

Farther on down the scene of desolation, Sue stopped in her tracks. "I don't believe this! A hotel?"

"A residence hotel, for old Jews and faded actors. As usual here in Venice, the inhabitants are a lot more colorful and better maintained than the architecture." Next door was a functioning grocery store. "There's another one down the block. They open alternate days, so we always have a place to get food for the beach."

Then there was nothing until Jan and Dee's Hamburgers. "They open about ten," Charles explained. "Off hours they run the Venice lesbian softball team." Charles stopped and pointed toward the sea. "If you go down to the water from here, you're on

Gay Beach, starting from that pile of rocks and going as far south as we need."

While Sue was digesting all of this, Ocean Front Walk dropped off into a broken roadway. "Welcome to Santa Monica," said Charles. He stopped in front of a short pier which looked as if you might be able to drive on it. At the end was an ancient tavern. "We have rock bands here on Sundays. It's free, but you pay for drinks."

When they reached the end of the tavern, Charles became very pensive. "And here you have Pacific Ocean Park."

"Jesus!" was all Sue could say. It wasn't really the old beach front amusement park with its rides and shows, POP, but the ruins of the businesses which had grown up around it. The paint was faded, signs were down, sides of the shacks were caved in, and everywhere there was trash. POP was an urban ghost town, terrifying because it was still occupied according to Charles—by indigents, junkies and various petty criminals.

"Here's where Danny found me."

"What on earth were you doing in a place like this? My god!"

They sat down there in the sand. "I wasn't fit for anywhere else. I had come back from Viet Nam after four years up-country with the Montanyards, and I couldn't even speak English any more. They let me go as soon as the plane landed, but I could have used about a year of therapy. I was having flashbacks all the time, and was a real danger to the community. It was a cold, rainy day and I was miserable and very hungry. Danny took me back home to her tiny apartment. She soaked me in the tub, fed me up on bowls of bulgar wheat and veggies. The upshot was, I got a GI loan; Danny figured she could make the payments somehow, and we got Highland House. Speaking of which, let's go home."

On the way home they passed another line of people a block long, entering through a glass door and up at least one story that Sue could see. "What happens at the other end of the line?" she inquired of Charles.

"Well," he said solemnly, "you tell the doctor what's wrong, and he prescribes any kind of controlled substance you happen to fancy. Then he phones downstairs to the drugstore, which he also owns, gives you a number, and you go down and get it with your MediCal sticker."

"This is the second place you stand in line?"

Charles nodded vehemently. "The third is Unemployment."

They retraced their steps to Highland House, which was at last alive with incumbents, overnight guests and hangers-on in various stages of dress and undress. Danny was 'dressed' in frayed blue jeans cut off five inches below the crotch and then rolled up a notch. For the time being she was preferentially bare-breasted.

The new rock station, KMET, came in through multiple radios giving a budget stereo effect from any place you stood. Everywhere the nutritious odors of late breakfast fused with incense and body oils. Chorizo competed unsuccessfully with patchouli as the Highland House denizens prepared for another afternoon at the beach.

Out in the front yard various shirts and pants dried in the light breeze, readying for the coming evening on the town. Patched and faded blue jeans, long too old to be stiff again, wafted in the brunch-time breeze. More conspicuous was a collection of sleeveless underwear, tie-dyed, silk-screened and air-brushed, which paled their store-bought imitations: bright-colored tank-tops with contrasting bias bindings on the necks and arm straps.

Floundering in the carnival atmosphere, Sue found Danny by listening for her voice. "Has anything been heard from Kim?" Sue asked. "Her spot in the hearse was cold all night."

"Kim took the bus to East El Lay last night."

"Why would anyone in L.A. take the bus? I thought everyone in L.A. had a car."

"Every place but in Venice and East L.A.," Danny explained. "Kim's with Flor. They should be back by noon, ready to go to the beach with everyone else."

"She doesn't waste any time, that one," said Sue.

"Kim only comes down here to play. It will take a few days for Patty to get someone to watch the store for her, but you can bet the Wicked Witch of the North will be burning up the pavement with that Ferrari of hers, and bring a bag of heroin, the one thing Kim can't pass up. In a few days Kim will be all strung out again. Patty will take her back to Stinson, and leave her all alone to kick by herself."

"I wish Kimmey would stay away from smack," Sue said, hoping to find an ally in Danny.

"She scares the hell out of me, wandering around when she's high. So far she's in one piece, but it's only a matter of time. All we can do is keep track of her until she slows down or learns to turn on at home."

"Do you think she's OK, way over in East L. A.?"

"Sure. With Flor around, Kim doesn't care to mess with anything as tame as hard drugs."

"Amazing, isn't it," said Sue, much less worried, "the effect those two have on each other!"

"You could call me a jaded old lady, as often as I've been around the block, but those two embarrass me. Anyhow, while Kim plays as fast as she can, I'm taking you over to Little Karen. She says she might have room for you."

"So soon! Man, you don't mess around!"

"It happens you're not the first in our unofficial case load around here. We need to hide away from our working friends, so they can't call us lazy, where we can live on little or nothing at all, and do a lot of drugs and booze and sex and keep healthy and feeling good until this recession is all over. With any luck we can keep each other alive until the Establishment either falls apart forever or gets busy."

"You mean people are actually dying? And I thought I was bad off, just being poor and out of work! All I need is to be warm and full and smoke a little pot sometimes. No other dope—I quit booze long ago."

"No booze? Good. If you can drive while the rest of us are still drunk or high, you can keep a lot of us alive and out of jail. It's time to split now. We'll move William Randolph over to Karen's before those thieves at the park have everything."

Danny picked up her beach towel, they slipped out the back door, through the gate and down the alley to the park where the hearse was still parked. Sue turned the key in the lock, and thought it felt funny. "Damn! It's unlocked already!"

25

"Hmm. Better take a good look around in there."

"Everything's still here…except my foot locker! Shit, they got all my clothes!" Sue was next to crying.

Danny took her gently by the upper arm and said, "Come on, let's go back to the house and smoke a couple of numbers and shine it on."

Sue could only nod and follow along. Upstairs in Danny's bedroom they lit up. Finally Sue dared to open her mouth. "It's not that there was anything valuable, it's just that it happens so often. When I went to Illinois I took only one suitcase, thinking I'd come back here to move properly when I got a job. The first month I was there, the finance company foreclosed on my house back home in Laguna Beach, took possession of it, and threw all my personal belongings in the Orange County Dump. I had just about got a few necessities together again, and had almost stopped missing certain things, and now those are gone!"

Danny started laughing. Then she said, "I'm sorry, Sue. I don't mean to make fun of your bad luck. These local thieves must think they're pretty slick, but you've been ripped off before, by the real experts!"

"Actually," said Sue, "the most expensive thing they got this time was the foot locker. Nothing I had cost much. Most of what I had was for winter in the East, and I need warm weather stuff now, anyway."

"I've got an extra twenty bucks. Let's go down to the Salvation Army and get you a new foot-locker and a bunch of new threads. You can pay me back some day."

"You'd do that for me?" said Sue, surprised.

"We have to keep up our reputation for looking good, don't we?"

"For sure, for sure." Sue was ready to smile again. When they got back to the hearse, she couldn't believe her eyes. "Would you look at that, Danny? It's back again!"

"Damned if it isn't!" The foot-locker was back in its usual place, but opened. "Have a look-see for what's missing."

Sue rummaged around for a while. "I can't believe it. Everything is here!"

They looked at each other, and started giggling. "I guess,"

said Danny, "they figured you're worse off than they are."

When they recovered their composure, Sue unlocked the front and got into the driver's seat. Danny got in the passenger's side and immediately turned for a solid stare in the back. "Man, this is classy! Where did you connect for a boat like this?"

Sue showed off the sound system while she explained, "William was the equipment truck for a Chicago rock band. The chill was pretty well worn off by the time I got it."

"It's the curtains," Danny solemnly announced. "Any color but black would make it more like a mere limousine. White or gray would be out of the question, though."

"I was thinking in terms of stripes or flowers."

"Far fuckin' out! I'll turn you on to the wholesale fabric place." Sue started the engine and they were off to Karen's.

They parked in front of a white, turn-of-the century Chinese-midwestern frame house on Rialto Street, a quiet avenue of family residences in the barrio. Karen occupied the second story of a house with a Mercedes in the driveway and a swarm of bicycles on the front lawn. The ground floor housed the land-lady, the beautiful and rich Marisol, a well-known fence for large-ticketed items. Her high-school-aged son, Jorge, was following in her footsteps, apprenticing with bicycles.

Concealed from the street and from the alley was a tiny one-room apartment on the ground floor. From the walkway it could be mistaken for a garage, which it might have been in some past life. But if you walked down a short, dead-end path you found a gate, a small sunny patio with several potted plants and the one door numbered Apt 1/2.

Little Karen's apartment was accessed from the driveway and up steep wooden stairs with heavy railings. Danny banged on the door lintel, and eventually a small, trim and smiling personage appeared through the beaded curtain. "Come on in. I'm making ice tea."

"I can't stay," said Danny. "I'll just leave you two to do your business." And she was gone, just like that. Little Karen laughed, shook her cropped mop of curly hair, and led Sue through the narrow cork-paneled kitchen into the twenty-foot living room. The heavy purple curtains were parted and the morning sun and sea breeze tumbled through the six-foot open windows on the heels of recorded Mariachi music from across the street. In the sunniest corner were a small stool, a burdened music rack and two saxophones, tenor and alto. The decor was mixed Medieval-Modern featuring an oriental rug of uncertain age and home-grown bunk beds, a square coffee table and a maroon mohair chair with crocheted antimacassars. Otherwise, sitting involved relating to one or more of many floor pillows.

Off the living room was an equally-large sun room which was Karen's bedroom. Snuggled next to it was a smaller bedroom with windows opening on the driveway. The bathroom was a center island with windows on two sides.

"I never know what to expect from Danny," said Karen.

"I think she was afraid we wouldn't like each other, and she'd be responsible," Sue ventured as she settled into the mohair chair.

"You're right! I hope she doesn't think we're getting married or something like that," Karen said. After a good laugh, which wrinkled her turned-up nose and added a flush to her tennis tan, she continued. "Actually, I've got an extra top bunk here. You're welcome to use it any time, that is if you don't mind Gary in the lower bunk. He's a really nice fag artist, and he's been around here from time to time for almost a year now."

"What kind of money are we talking about here?" asked Sue, mindful of her limited resources.

"Let's see. My rent for this whole mansion is only a hundred dollars a month, half of which I get from Chris, in the real bed-room over there. We won't see much of Chris. She comes in only after work to change clothes and go to her old lady's for dinner and sex. Your share of the floor space is eighteen square feet, the size of the bunk, which you share with Gary in the lower. Divide that by two is nine square feet, which brings your share to five dollars, which I would feel silly collecting. So I can't charge you any rent."

By then Sue was laughing hard. "I can see I'm going to have trouble with you, with all that impeccable arithmetic! Why would you not want to charge me rent?"

"You see all this furniture and stuff?" Karen passed a hand

28

across the horizons of her realm. "I gave the previous resident one busted old van for possession of the apartment and all its contents, so it was really free. As we say in Venice, 'What goes around comes around.' For another thing, the gay community is getting very solid all over California. When we go up to San Francisco, for instance, we can count on having some place to stay, so long as we have sleeping bags. We all help each other."

"It seems like everyone is contributing what she can. Danny says that having my hearse and being sober enough to drive when everyone else has passed out will be a valuable service."

"Danny's right. You might as well know right now," said Karen a bit embarrassed. "I'm something of a drunk. I'm not mean or messy. I just sit there smiling quietly and finally pass out. Giving up my van probably saved my life. Knowing that you'll be around to get me home safe and tucked in will be great peace of mind."

Sue laughed. "If you're too drunk to lead around, I'll have to tuck you into the guest sleeping bag in the hearse, if that's OK with you."

"As one ex-urban camper to another, on sunny mornings it's not half bad waking up in a vehicle." After a long pause, Karen continued. "So there you are. The only reservation is, you might get bumped out temporarily when my brother Steven is home from the sea twice a year. So what do you say, roommate?"

"I say OK!" said Sue.

"Well far fuckin' out!" They sealed the deal with ice tea and a fat joint.

As Sue sat stirring her tea she felt something warm and wet at the back of her knee. She looked around into the proud but playful face of a white and spotted whippet, a small racing dog bred for speed, intelligence and a sense of humor. "And here," continued Karen, "we have Toots, the most important person in the family. Since she's been fixed, her only vices are running, and chewing up anything interesting. Do you think you and Toots can work up a deal?" With that, Toots sat upright on the floor, with her front paws tucked up into her groin, hoping to appear as small as possible.

"What do you say, Toots?" Sue said.

"She says she's in love," Karen whispered.

About noon Karen set out for the beach, and Sue went along as far as the Safeway. She returned home with an arm load of orange juice and Fritos settling into the bath tub for this foolish feast. How long had she been without a real bath, in a real tub? A year? Sure, there had been plenty of saunas at Kim's and hurried showers one place or another, but seldom the luxury of a hot soak. She munched and scrubbed until the water cooled. Then she dried and crashed in the top bunk until Karen and Toots with someone imposing came from the beach in fine spirits.

When the girls had shaken the sand out of their clothes, Sue raised her head over the bed rails and waved wearily so they wouldn't feel they had to whisper in Karen's own house.

"Sue, meet Nola," Karen offered.

"Well, hello again! I wish you and the Kim had stayed around Stinson a little longer," Nola crooned. What Sue saw from her perch on the top bunk was Nola's long, tan face with its simply beautiful smile in a waterfall of golden hair. "This is the last time you get to sleep through beach-time," said Nola. "Everyone was asking about you, and refused to believe you're home here in bed...alone!"

Sue moistened her leathery-dry mouth for a reply. "As my press agent you need to know that I can be a terrible disappointment in the afternoon."

Nola rumpled Sue's mouse-brown hair and massaged her soul with her bright blue eyes. "I'll keep that in mind while I spread it around how good you look naked."

With that, Sue was more than just awake. "Either hand me my cut-offs, or come up here yourself." From across the room Karen heard that remark and let the cut-offs fly like an unravelling fast-pitch softball. Having thus defined the situation, they all had a good laugh while Sue pulled and zippered herself into presentability.

Sue swung her legs over the rail and landed on the floor. "Can't put it off any longer. Got to go down to William Randolph for the aspirin and the toothache kit. I've got this molar with a hole the size of my head, and no money to get it fixed or pulled."

Nola wet her two forefingers on her tongue, smoothed her brown eyebrows and tried to look smug. "I get all my dental work free."

"You have a close relative in dentistry?"

"Nope. The UCLA Free Dental Clinic up on Lincoln Avenue. I'll take you with me to my next appointment in a couple of weeks. You sit in line now and again, but they really are free, and it's the best work in the world."

"Free dentistry! That would solve one of my worst problems, and help with all the rest!"

"When it comes to getting or saving money, take lessons from Nola," said Little Karen. "She gets Unemployment and Disability and works two jobs. I think she still has the first nickel she ever earned."

"Nope," said Nola. "My first nickel I spent on a piggy bank. Now, if you'll get me that cold beer you promised, I'll be on my way to my night-time job."

Chapter 5

After delivering the beer to Nola and Nola to the door, Karen came back with a box of zip-lock baggies, a scale, and a heavy-looking paper bag. With a flourish, she emptied out the contents of the paper bag into the mohair chair and then drew the purple velvet drapes across the front windows. "At last!" she shouted in a whisper "I got my grass!" Sure enough, there were two brown bricks wrapped in plastic. "Sometimes I think the big dealers make us wait just to keep the price inflated. Will you help me with this? Then I can get it out of sight faster."

"Sure. What are we going to do?" Suddenly Sue felt like the raw recruit she really was.

"Danny didn't that mention I'm a dealer?" Karen asked. We're going to break these kis into one-ounce bags.

"Aren't you afraid of getting caught?"

"Not with the little bit I'm doing these days. Uppers and downers and grass is nothing compared to what I was doing at Douglas Aircraft. Me and my boss were dealing out of the tool crib. I had a roving pass so I could make deliveries by roller skates. Both of us got scared about the time we got rich and quit."

Sue laughed. "When I was at North American I used to wonder why life was so mellow on night shift. What will you get for those bags?"

"I think ten bucks a lid, as usual. We don't aim to retire, just keep enough grass for ourselves."

"I'll open each baggie and hand it to you. You weigh and stuff it and I'll close and put it back in the paper bag."

"Go!" said Karen. In half an hour they were finished, and

Karen had stuffed the full paper bag into a hole in the living room wall, conveniently and tastefully covered with a small tapestry. "Now, all you have to do is keep your mouth shut in certain places."

The morning after the two kis had been bagged and stashed Karen went to play paddle tennis with Nola. Someone came knocking while Sue was still luxuriating in bed after another whole night indoors. She rolled out of bed fully dressed from the day before, still not over habits learned sleeping in a vehicle.

She opened the door on a complete stranger. "Is Karen here?" he asked.

"She's at the paddle tennis courts, if you want to see her."

"I'm San Francisco Bart."

"I'm Sue. Hey, aren't you a friend of Rickey's, at Maude's?"

"Yeh. So you're Sue? I've heard about you."

"Why don't you come in and wait a few minutes. Karen and Nola will be back soon," Sue suggested.

Bart shuffled, as if he was about to go away. Then, as if a new idea dawned on him, he stepped inside and said, "Sure. I guess I can wait a few minutes." He set himself in the mohair chair and had a good look around. "Groovy place she has here. Actually, what I want is to buy a lid. Maybe you could sell me one?"

"Sure. Ten dollars." Sue was glad to do Karen a favor. She would be pleased with an easy ten dollars.

Bart handed over a ten dollar bill. Sue pulled aside the little tapestry and extracted a lid, leaving the money in its place. He opened the baggie and inhaled deeply. "Ah, what a lovely smell! Say, is that coffee I smell, too? How about a cup for the road?"

"Sure." When she got back from the kitchen, Bart had vanished, gone without leaving a trace! She sat in the mohair chair and drank the coffee herself, contemplating this strange event.

Soon enough, the racket of Nola's chopped Honda motorcycle filled the driveway. Karen and Nola appeared in a morning sweat and ready for the first beer of the day. "By the way," said Sue from the mohair chair. "San Francisco Bart was here."

"Bart? What in hell did he want?" Karen asked.

"He wanted to buy a lid."

"That heavy dealer? Wanted a lid?" Nola and Karen looked at each other in a flash of incomprehension.

"So I sold him one. A person can always use an extra dime. I hope that was OK," said Sue with the sudden and profound feeling that it was not OK. She told them the whole story.

After 'true confessions,' Sue felt relieved but somehow apprehensive as Karen asked "He saw you go into the stash?" Sue nodded. Karen and Nola turned white and simultaneously dove for the hole in the wall. Sue's heart sank as her new friends settled back onto the floor and stared at each other.

Karen was the first to speak. "Gone! Every scrap gone! Damn it, Nola, that slime-bag got my whole stash—Grass, pills, money and all! Out the window, over the roof like some god damned Santa Claus, smooth as railroad chili!"

Nola shook her head and stared at Sue in disbelief. "How can a smart person like you be so stupid?"

"He really fooled me." Sue was near to tears, but managed to save them all the indignity of watching her cry. "You've been so good to me since I came to town, and then I let you down like this. I don't know what I can do."

Karen tried to be nice. "We'll just shine it on, Sue. You'll be surprised how fast we'll make it back."

Nola wasn't smiling. Turning to her, Karen advised, "Don't be so hard on Sue. She'll get some street smarts. The main thing is, what are we going to do now?"

Nola dialed as she spoke. "What we always do, Little Karen. Call in the Maaa-fia...Danny? This is Nola. We need you over here at Karen's, A.S.A.P."

Because she was in training for softball, Danny ran from Highland House to Karen's in two minutes and came in huffing. "How long has he been gone? Wait till I get a hold of that fucker!"

"It happened a couple of hours ago."

"He got my whole stash, damn him!"

"No use chasing after him now."

Sue was in tears. "It's all my fault. I'm so dumb sometimes. What are we going to do?"

"Do?" said Danny, shaking with determination. "We're going

to make him pay for this one way or another, through the nose or worse!"

"Well all *right!*" hollered Nola, ready for anything.

"Sue, will that hearse of yours make it to San Francisco and back?" Danny asked.

"Sure, easy. It still averages fifty miles an hour. What for?"

"Yeah, what for?" asked Karen. By now the thrill of adventure and the promise of vengeance had made a new person of her.

Danny swelled with determination. "We're going to San Francisco to kidnap Juice."

"Bart's little sister! And the ransom is my stash! Shazam!" said Karen.

"Correctomundo!" said Danny proudly.

An incredulous Nola objected. "I don't get it. Why would he care enough to pay that much ransom for his little teen-aged sister? Maybe he'll be glad to get rid of her. You don't know what jerks big brothers can be."

Danny rebutted. "You should see how nice she keeps his apartment, and what a good cook Juice is. Don't worry, he'll want his life style back again."

Nola shifted her weight in the mohair chair, looking for a different angle of attack. "OK. If Juice is such a prize, how are we going to get her away from him in the first place?"

"Like, Juice won't cooperate?" said Danny, almost too pleased with herself to blush.

"That's right! You dog, you! I remember you and Juice on our Exmas trip north," Nola said, giving Danny an elbow in the ribs. "Let's go!"

They stopped at Highland House for Danny's city clothes and found Kim in an uneasy funk. "I can feel Patty fifteen miles away. That means she's in town and closing in on me!"

Danny gave her a rabbit punch on the arm. "So grab your underwear and go get in the hearse. We're on the way to San Francisco! Patty will never think of looking for you so near Stinson Beach, and we need someone strong of mind and body."

In fifteen minutes the hearse was gassed up and on the freeway, Kim and Danny sprawled in the back compartment, Karen and Nola in front, keeping Sue awake and plied with coffee and mini-bennies. "What the hell are we going to Frisco for, anyway?" asked Kim, almost afraid to question her good luck for the ride.

"We're going to kidnap Juice."

"Juice? My little friend, Jail Bait! Why are we kidnapping Juice?"

"Because San Francisco Bart ripped off Karen's stash, and because I need somebody new, that's why," summarized Danny Mae.

"That will do for some excitement, all right," said Kim. After several minutes of silent contemplation, she came out with it. "I've got news for you. I'm in love with Flor."

Danny sat bolt upright. "You're in *what* with *who*?"

"*Love* with *Flor*."

"Sweet Jesus! Evelyn's girl!"

"Do I ever do anything simply?" asked Kim just before she fell sound asleep.

Two bennies later, Sue pulled into a secluded parking lot in Golden Gate Park. Danny's raspy voice came though the morning air, "I'm starving."

"I think there are some ancient graham crackers in the larder," said Sue.

"Larder?"

"The three-foot can with a 'LARD' label pasted on it. You can't miss it." Then she crashed out with the engine running.

Some time later she stirred as a metallic, mechanical coughing assailed her ears, but she thought nothing of it and sank back into oblivion. As the sun rose, Kim slid in beside her and whispered, "I found your gas can. Have you got any rubber tubing?"

Sue awakened so fast you would have thought her brain exploded. "Shit, man! You mean I let this crate run out of gas?" Kim nodded and giggled, as Sue continued. "Look in the storage box over the driver's cab."

"There's a car parked all alone over there, and the tank is unlocked," said Kim before gum-shoeing off through the gravel.

In ten minutes William Randolph had a breakfast snack, and Kim slid into the passenger's seat with the can smelling of gas.

"Could you just hold that thing out the window for a little while?" Sue pleaded.

"Better yet." Kim hung the can handle over the radio antenna, and stuffed the rubber pipe into it. "Maybe I should have put some of that in the carb."

"It always pumps up enough. Just pray for enough battery." After a couple of good tries the engine turned over, and they backed out into the road. "Now I believe the Great Beyond is down to earth."

When they pulled into the cheapie station, the load of suntan in the back came to life with compound goose-pimples. They pulled on their sweatshirts and warmed in William Randolph's cozy midst. "Where are we going?" Nola wanted to know as they turned onto Lincoln Ave.

"Just keep on going," said Danny. "Juice lives with her brother, over on Frederick Street, around the corner from Maude's Bar."

"I have to eat before anything like that," squeaked poor starving Karen.

"If I eat before beer I throw up," Nola groaned. Out of proper respect for Nola's tender gastronomy as well as the upholstery, Sue pulled over to a grocery with a flickering beer sign. Everyone found something they liked in cellophane, paper or glass. "What we need is a troop leader," said Nola from the bottom of her beer bottle. "Since Danny knows everything, I vote for Danny."

Danny and the mob staked out San Francisco Bart and Juice's Frederick Street apartment and waited all morning without seeing him leave. "We better do something fast," said Kim. "I have to tell you, I'm losing my nerve."

"Well, I sure can't make Bart get out of there."

"Hmm. Do you know his phone number?" said Kim.

"If it's the same as Juice's, I know it," said Danny. "That's it. Let's call Juice and ask for Bart. She doesn't know your voice, Kim. Or does she?"

They rolled up to a phone booth, and extruded Kimmey. She was back quicker than expected and announced, "Bart's on his way back from La-La Land. The coast is clear."

Knocking on the front door the way they did, they could have been delivering Avon orders instead of abducting Juice. Juice answered the door herself. There she stood, all fifteen years of her, in her tank top with her tanned belly button boldly visible above an oversized pair of white track shorts. "Danny! I thought you'd never come back!" said Juice as she backed Danny into a corner.

Finally Danny recovered her authority. "We're kidnapping you to Venice, so you'd better get packing."

Juice laughed. "Kidnapping? You have a willing victim."

Before leaving town the Maa-fia stopped off at Maude's Bar to cheer their successful snatching. Rickey shook her head decisively. "You know I can't let Juice in here anymore. She's jail bait. If the law catches me serving someone that young I'll risk going to jail and losing my license."

"Look," said Kimmey, "It isn't every day we have a kidnapping to celebrate, and we won't be here long. Just a few for the road?"

"Well, OK, just this once. But you better hurry and get in here before anyone sees you." Rickey glanced furtively up and down Cole Street where housewives were dashing into the delis, students were rushing in and out of the groceries, fags were waiting for chow fu gunk at the Chinese next door, and cops were writing out tickets for cars parked in the bus zone.

Once inside, the Maa-fia rubbed their eyes to adjust to the dark. Then Sue's heart jumped a beat, raced into her throat and dropped dead. She recognized a plump and scrubbed brunette. Yazmina! Alone at the end of the bar!

Yaz caught Sue in her peripheral vision, did a double take, and came running. With her arms around Sue's neck she whispered. "You're back at last!"

"Just for the day, Yaz. It looks like I've moved to L.A. more or less permanently. Would you care to dance with an older woman?" With no more ado they were on the small dance floor by the pool table. The sudden rush to Sue's gonads made her knees go weak and her tongue turn to cold lead. She knew she had less than three minutes to get her and Yaz out into the back patio before she crashed.

It was a photo finish. Later on she wouldn't remember the slump near the bar, the karoom around the door and the final crash into the canvas chair. Yaz went racing to Kim for help. "Something is wrong with Sue. You better come help me with her."

Kim pushed back Sue's eye-lids looking for the light of life, but stopped all that technical stuff in the face of an extended snore. "Sue has narcolepsy. She passes out when she gets over-excited."

"Come on, then," said Yaz, who couldn't let a good thing pass. "Let's wake her up, quick."

"That's impossible. She has to wake up by herself, maybe in about half an hour."

Danny was looking over Yaz's head. "By now Rat Bart is probably back home and has read our ransom note. We better load Sue into William Randolph and split before Bart and his heavies catch us here with no reinforcements and take us apart."

Kim was looking glum. "I'll bet he'll be calling Patty at Highland House, and they'll be looking for us from both directions at once."

"Will you block-heads come back to reality?" Nola exclaimed.

"First off, Bart won't know we've got Juice until he gets back to Frisco and reads the note we left on his door. As for Patty, at the rate she moves it will be days before she comes back here."

"So we're safe," said Kim in a better mood, "for a few days. Why don't we party at Stinson? Bart will never think of looking for us there."

Danny relaxed her leadership role. "Someone says *party* and I say *yeah*! The only thing we have to do is get back to Venice before the curtain rises four days from now. Will someone get a hold of Sue's feet? I can't load this dead weight all by myself, you know." Juice picked up Sue's feet, one under each arm, and she and Nola marched toward the door.

"I don't get it," said Kimmey. "What's the big rush? What's all this about the curtain rising?"

"That's right," said Danny. "You haven't been around since

the rock opera opened at the Venice Pavilion, down on the beach. Karen's in love with the contralto star. If we leave Stinson two days from now, after breakfast, we'll be on time."

"Well then, what are we waiting for?" said Kim as she started the engine.

After Juice and Nola had loaded Sue in through the corpse door and laid her out in the coffin spot, Juice remarked to anyone who cared to hear, "I've lost track; who's the abduc*tor* and who's the abduc*tee* around here?"

With Kim's sure and experienced hand on the wheel, Nola soon snoozed in the co-pilot's seat, while in the back Danny and Juice cuddled in the noontime sun. Next to them Sue slept soundly, not stirring until the stones in the gravel from Stinson's main drag clattered around in William Randolph's wheel wells. She opened one sleepy eye, and then the other when she recognized the face not two inches from her own. "Yaz! What the…. Are you coming back to Venice with us?"

"Hush. We're in Stinson for a couple of days. Patty will never think of looking for Kim out here."

Sue's lips formed a questioning reply but found it impeded by a soft, long kiss after which she forgot any objection she might have entertained.

They were parked inside the fence at Kimmey's (Patty's) house, and Nola was saying, "Just leave those love birds alone. Eventually they'll figure out we've gone surfing." More than willing to play the game, Sue and Yaz didn't move until their friends' footsteps vanished in the distance.

"Come on then," Yaz whispered into Sue's ear. "Down to my cabin. If they can't find us, so much the better."

Scarcely believing the fantastic change in her luck, Sue could only nod in reply and speak in practicalities. "There's a tooth brush in the compartment over the driver's cab." When it was safely in hand, they got out the co-pilot's side of the hearse and pulled the door closed as quietly as a bank vault. The gate to the compound slid into place on the fence posts and they were on their way down to Yaz's Peachbottom Flat.

Hand in hand they walked the half mile. As soon as their feet crunched in the gravel a small striped cat heard them and trotted to meet Yaz. He was allowed to ride on her shoulder the rest of the way home. Once inside Yaz lit two fat aromatic candles to reveal the tidy but simple appointments of her raw-wood cabin. She plopped the cat on the rag throw-rug and said to Sue, "If you'll grab a couple of armloads of stove-lengths from that pile by the porch, and build a fire in the Franklin stove, I'll feed this neglected, deprived individual."

The chores done, Yaz dipped water from the bucket into the blackened pot on the stove. The cat, soon fed and happy, sat cleaning her impeccable self at the window, boldly open to the crisp ocean air.

While they waited for coffee they hung their jackets over the chair, kicked off their sneakers and stretched out beside each other on the patchwork comforter. Cooled by the ocean breeze and by contrast warmed by the radiating stove and Yaz beside her, Sue looked into those black Persian eyes with the candle light flickering in them. It was Yaz's soft, Danish half that pushed Sue over the brink of whatever had held her back before.

It was so easy kissing Yaz. When she finally stopped and recovered, there was the wildest suggestion being whispered into her ear. "Please make love to me, Sue. I've never had sex with anyone before, and I really trust you. Please?"

"You mean," said the surprised Sue, "You're a *virgin?*"

"It comes down to that," Yaz confessed, almost ashamed.

"At the age of...?"

"Twenty-six."

Sue definitely needed time to collect herself. "I need to go to the toilet and I need an aspirin."

"The bathroom is in its usual place."

As soon as Sue opened the medicine cabinet she was back, with a puzzled look on her face and, in her hand, a plastic card with thirty or so pills in a circle, several missing. "If you're really a virgin, why in hell do you have birth control pills?"

"I can always hope, can't I?"

"Yaz, honey," said Sue as she stepped into her sneakers, "I always make it a point never to fuck anyone who hasn't at least got something like the hots for me and vice versa."

"You must think I'm terrible," said Yaz in a lowered voice.

"Not at all. I think we're both prudes, and there's very little hope for either one of us."

"I'll tell you what," said Yaz, hugging Sue. "I'll hit on you again when I manage to get through this extended adolescence."

"For you, I could even wait around." Sue gave her a determined sisterly kiss which felt so good she gave her another with different meaning, and still another which sealed their fate for the foreseeable future.

"I think," said Yaz, "adolescence is over."

"It's a good thing I've just slept, or I'd crash right now."

"I'd wake you up soon enough—except I don't know exactly what to do. Making love, I mean."

"It's so easy you won't believe it. You just enjoy what happens, and do whatever you feel like doing."

"I feel like getting naked," said Yaz. "You know how I like being naked."

"As it happens, I like you being naked, too." Soon they were standing on a pile of socks, then the T-shirts, and then their jeans were down around their knees, the ankles, the feet.

Their bodies felt so good held close together like that. "I think we should be lying down," said Sue. Together still, they sank onto the patchwork quilt, warm in the noontime sun. "Sex is so good in the sunshine."

"Will you shut-the-fuck-up?" said Yaz in her husky Persian whisper. "I can't pay attention with all this talk!" She kissed Sue's mouth just to be sure. There was touching and kneading and, as Sue moved into the space made for her between Yaz's legs and rested her hand in the warmth, there was a moving and erecting of the clitoris. Yaz caught her breath. "What's going on down there?"

"You mean you never learned to masturbate?"

"I haven't felt anything like this since we learned to climb the ropes in gym class."

Sue boldly slipped two fingers into Yaz's vagina. She stopped suddenly when she felt something like a loop of clothesline wire. Some instinct from the past said "Pull." There was a springing sensation, and she had a round frame of wire with a film of rubber across.

"A diaphragm?" Sue exclaimed.

"I told you I'm always prepared."

Sue began giggling and they shook with laughter as Yaz tossed the thing into the trash basket, like a miniature frisbee. Meanwhile, back to the business at hand, Sue was impressed with the abundance of creative juice. "You are either the most provident Girl Scout or the sexiest virgin in town," Sue observed

"A nursing education is good for something."

That was all anyone said for some time, including a sound and satisfying sleep in each other's arms. When they awoke they could hear Kim's laughter and Danny's raucous voice from the Sand Dollar Bar across the street. The gentle clonk of pool balls accounted for Karen, Nola and Juice. While their friends were so nicely distracted, Sue and Yaz dressed minimally and sneaked over to Ed's Superette for enough eggs, hamburger, bread and orange drink to last a couple of days.

Eventually the hearse pulled up in front of Peachbottom and honked. Between the wet and tearful good-bye kisses Yaz wanted to know "When are you coming back?"

"I don't know, honey. I've got to see about making some money before I can think about taking another vacation."

"Remember when I did your Tarot? I guess we know now that all that love and money is for *you!*"

"After the past few days I'll believe in anything," said Sue. "In the meantime, while my pot of gold is on its way, you could truck on down to Venice once in a while."

"What a plan! And we can write letters."

They clasped hands and walked bravely to face the whistles and cat calls of their friends. While Yaz held the cab door open, Sue slid into the driver's seat, and the kidnapping resumed.

Nola and Little Karen slid into the co-pilot's seat leaving Danny and Juice to slump and doze as AM turned to PM. When the yacht dropped anchor in Coalinga for gas, Juice stuck her hand into Danny's front pocket and came up not only with an attentive groan but a dollar bill, good for two cans of Coors.

Juice opened Danny's hand and inserted a new, cold beer. Danny opened one blue eye and smiled.

"Hi, Chief," said Juice.

"Hi, Rug-Rat," said Danny.

"What makes you think my yucky brother is going to pay ransom money for me, of all people?"

"He doesn't have to give money. He can just return Karen's stash."

"Now you're for sure hallucinating! If you want to know the truth, he'll be glad to be rid of me." Tough little Juice was downright sad.

"I don't believe it. If he wanted to be rid of you, he would have sent you back to your mother," said Danny.

"But we have no idea what happened to her. When I ran away, she and that old man of hers split so far it will take the FBI to find them."

"He could have turned you over to the Juvenile Authority."

"But didn't," Juice said emphatically. "The Authority would have gone through his place like a dose of Exlax."

"Whatever," said Danny as she gave Juice a comforting hug. "You're better off down in Venice with us. As for Karen's stash— as soon as we get home, I'll get hold of my connection and pony up for a new load. I always did want a kid like you."

Chapter 6

The Maa-fia got back to Venice in plenty of time for the opening curtain at half past eight. Nola was there early with a load of Cokes and burritos, and slipped into the seat next to Sue, saving Karen's usual place in the stands. "So tell me about the show," said Sue.

"I guess you were still out cold when I gave Kim the word," said Nola. "It's kind of a rock opera about life here in Venice. This guy in town wrote it all, and the whole cast lives here, too. They have been giving it rave reviews in the *Los Angeles Times*, and people have been coming out from town to see it—more every week. It only runs weekends, and will quit in three more weeks. It's a swell show, for a freebee! The biggest thing is, Karen's in love with the star."

Little Karen slipped in at eight-twenty with the rush of the main crowd. She settled next to Nola on the aisle seat with a clear view of the spot from which the contralto star of the show would be singing her main songs, the two best in the show.

Shortly before the first intermission the object of Karen's affection, three hundred pounds of flesh and caftan and four feet of braided chestnut hair, swept in from the wings and covered the white X on the floor. The stage lights dimmed, the spotlight came on, the bongo chorus stopped, and one guitar began the background for a love song about *You Always Stay So Far Above Me And Vanish Into Thin Air When I Go To Find You*.

The background faded to black, and two children in local batik and air-brushed motif came onto the stage with a sign announcing Intermission. The house lights came on and the bustle began, but the three musketeers sat there sighing.

Finally Sue broke the silence. "What's she like, Karen?"

"Go ahead and tell her," Nola said softly.

After a few pensive moments Karen confessed, "I've never met her."

While the two Venice Regulars watched in stunned disbelief, Sue rose without a word, walked toward the stage and disappeared through a door at orchestra level promising entrance to the actors' domain. Once inside she slipped in among the costumes and musical instruments and navigated to ground zero.

"Excuse me, miss," Sue said softly. "A girl friend of mine in the audience is dying to meet you, but is too bashful to come back here. Would you let me introduce you?"

"Oh! Is it by any chance that darling little woman in the brown fedora and leather vest? I thought I was going to have to wait forever!"

And so it was arranged. Sue got back to her seat just as the music started. She whispered to Karen, just loud enough for Nola to hear, too. "Go backstage afterward. Sylvia will take you to the cast party with her."

Karen watched the last act in high anticipation, and Sue began to believe that one way or another she would eventually make up for the stolen stash whether or not Bart ever paid Juice's ransom.

By five o'clock the next evening Karen had polished her boots and cleaned a lid of grass from the new ki Danny and Juice brought over. While her bath water was running she had her books out and was doing her numerology and astrology. "One of these days I've got to ask Cherry to teach me to do Tarot cards."

"Then all that will be left for you to learn is phrenology and scapulamancy," said Sue.

"Phrenology: That's how to read the bumps on your head. But I never heard of the other."

"Scapulamancy," Sue repeated. "If you get the shoulder bone of a deer and roast it over an open fire, it will get tiny cracks all over it. It's a lot like reading tea leaves."

"Now you're making fun of me," said Karen, smiling. "But it's all true. You'll see."

"What do you need all this good luck for, anyway? It seems to me things are going pretty well...except for the stolen stash, that is," said Sue.

"Never mind about the stash, Sue. Danny staked me to a new load, and I'll get it all paid back in two weeks."

"Did Danny really do that?" said Sue. "The gesture was as much for me as for you, I figure."

"Speaking of good luck," said Karen, " I'm having dinner with Gary and Nickey. Then I've got a real date with Sylvia tonight, after the show."

"I wonder if there's magic for narcolepsy? I could sure use some, huh?"

"I'll ask Cherry if you want. Anyhow, up north there's someone who's not going to care about a little thing like narcolepsy."

"Whatever," said Sue, rather lonesome. "One of us has a date tonight, anyhow."

"Pull up a pillow. I'll do a short-short astrology for you. Scorpio?"

"Scorpio," Sue confirmed, not at all sure she wanted any of this.

Karen did something with two books, pencil and paper. "I've never seen so much money! Need I say, this is a good year for business? But what's all this love and death? It's all around you, but doesn't involve you. I don't understand."

"Think nothing of it, roommate. The cards said the same thing about me to Yaz, and she didn't believe it either. If I believed any of it, I'd leave town."

About eight o'clock Sue was settled in bed with the new issue of *Scientific American*, never expecting the phone to ring, but it did. "This is Gary. I'm right outside the show, and you'd better come over and get Karen."

"What's wrong with Karen," Sue asked, terrified.

"Nothing much. She had too much wine at dinner and just sat down and passed out on the grass outside the show."

Just then two girls from the neighborhood burst in the door. "Are you Karen's new roommate? Come help us! Some black man has got a hold of Karen!"

Still on the phone Sue shrieked at Gary. "Idiot! Now you've

done it! I think you could take a little better care of your friends!" Then she hung up and ran along with the girls to the scene of the crime. Down at the corner a crowd had begun to collect to watch. To Sue's relief, the black man was Charles from Highland House, a good friend of Karen's. He was carrying her to her house where she ought to be, drunk as she was. Every so often Karen woke up frightened, staring into a face she didn't recognize at such close quarters, and she would punch and flail until he dropped her on the ground. In a huff she would stand up, brush herself off and immediately fall over, drunk and out cold again. Charles would pick her up again, and the whole show would repeat itself.

Sue said to Charles, "You've sure got your hands full."

"For such a little one she can be a problem."

"Maybe if each of us took an arm we could lead her," Sue suggested.

Charles shook his head. "It's sure worth a try."

When they had Karen on her feet again, they found themselves facing two ominous but determined Mexicans, one with a ball bat, the other with a rifle, walking swiftly to Karen's rescue. An electric hush flooded the vicinity.

Carefully, Sue let go of Karen and walked toward the 'posse.' "Karen's OK. Me and Charles are taking her home where she can sober up. Thanks for helping, but she's almost home."

Just then two black-and-white police cars wheeled around the corner, sirens blaring. After they stopped, four uniformed cops got out with guns drawn. The crowd gasped. One of the policemen demanded, "What's going on here?"

Sue had the presence of mind to step forward and say, "My roommate is a little drunk. Everyone is just trying to help."

To everyone's relief the pistols went back into their holsters. However, they had to justify their drawn guns and arrest someone for something or lose face. Who did they insist on taking away? Charles of course. No one seemed to be able to talk them out of cuffing him and prodding him into the back seat of the black-and-white, and hauling him of to the Venice Division Station.

After losing Karen at the pavilion, Gary and Nickey showed

up in time to follow the police to the station, bail Charles out, and bring him back to Karen's.

Karen was sober by the final curtain, in time for her date with Sylvia.

Juice and friend

Chapter 7

The next morning Sue awakened with the general impression that someone nearby had just turned over. She raised her head to have a look around: it was Gary, still in his boxer shorts and socks, groping around the living room for a cigarette.

"There's a fresh pack in my jacket, over the chair," Sue croaked. "You could hand me one, too."

"You're a lifesaver! You can have your coffee in bed, if you want, or you can come out into the sun with me and Daisy."

"That's a lot to digest, right away. Yes to coffee in the sun. Who's Daisy?"

She's David's cat, next door, and an old friend."

"I can't believe I've been thrashing around up here in my bare skin," said Sue. "It proves how fast I can get used to sleeping indoors. How about tossing me my jeans and T-shirt, also on the chair."

When they were settled on the steps among Karen's potted pot plants with Daisy and Toots keeping order, Gary said, "I think we should be more quiet. Karen came in early this morning, followed by something very large."

"Then she scored with Sylvia?"

"Well, it's about time. You girls sure spar around a lot before you get down to it."

"We're a bunch of prudes. How about a morning walk?"

Gary shook his head. "On any other day, but not today. Nickey the Easter Bunny is coming over. He promised he would let me draw him."

While Gary waited around for his drawing appointment, Sue walked down to the beach with Toots. As she stepped off the

50

walkway onto the sand somewhere between Jan and Dee's Hamburgers and the rock-pile on gay beach she overheard voices coming from a blanket. "What I like most about weekends is that I don't have to feel guilty about not looking for a job."

Amused by that homily, she sat down to watch the early morning gay and lesbian surfers. While Toots chanced the smaller waves, Sue contemplated. There was really only one problem—money. But it was so big it seemed insurmountable. How to get money? Where to earn it? She once believed she had answered that question for a lifetime by earning her way with her brain and her pencil. Now none of that was any good.

But maybe she had other alternatives? She *had* deliberately learned not to type over forty words per minute, thus saving herself from typing for a living—a good enough plan when one is young and has lots of possibilities. Enough rotten truth for one sunny day. Rotten. She contemplated her tooth ache as she headed back home.

Home at last, Sue heard male voices on the roof. She stepped off the stairs, onto the ladder and across the eaves. Both Gary and Nickey were substantially naked except for sun glasses, but not disturbed by her presence. "Inspection time," she said. "Let's see how you draw." It was the likeness of Nickey all right, each line meticulously drawn.

"Is there a market for art?" Sue had sudden inspiration.

"I manage," said Gary.

"And so do I," said Nickey, "and nicely. Crafts are where the bucks are, though," he said, understanding they were looking for a livelihood for Sue.

Gary pointed with his pencil in the direction of his jeans jacket. "See what's in the pocket."

Curious, Sue came up with a beautiful integration of beads and string. "What's this?"

"That's macrame, a key fob, with a hook to attach it to your belt loop. Three dollars. Very handy. Very hip."

Nickey got into it then. "The big crafts scene is a fair in Westwood on Friday and Saturday nights. There's a little alcove there, a block or so south of the Village Deli."

"Ah, yes. The VD. I was a grad student at UCLA."

"The craftspeople set up their sales tables at five-thirty, but the best time to snoop around is after the movies are out at ten o'clock. No one wants to go home yet, so they are ready to draw down their net spendable. You can get a good idea what sells and what doesn't."

"You know," said Sue. "When I was a kid I never could draw, but I did have a flair for crafts. How about going along to Westwood?" The guys looked longingly at each other and shook their heads. "So I'll go ask Karen!"

"Don't count on her," said the guys in unison.

Sue climbed down from the eaves and stood in the kitchen. When the sun was rubbed from her eyes she saw before her the overwhelming hulk of Big Sylvia with Little Karen nestled in her rigging.

"Thanks to you, I'm moving in," Sylvia announced.

"Well congratulations, you two!"

"I had almost given up on my shy honey here," continued Sylvia. "Thank heaven you had some good sense, Sue."

Before Sue got used to the situation herself, a blonde woman, presumably Chris whom no one had seen in weeks, stormed out of her room. "Jesus! I can't stand these crowds! I'm packing my shit and I'm leaving!" She slammed the door behind her, and continued boxing her shit for the big move.

As soon as the slam stopped rattling the windows, Karen recovered her senses and assumed command over her small but over-crowded empire. "After all this time, and she leaves me with a mailbox full of billmies."

"What, pray tell, is or are billmies?" asked Sue.

"Well," Karen explained, "if you read the magazine ads, the record clubs and book publishers have coupons for you to send in to get their best sellers regularly at a substantial price reduction. You fill in name and address, and put an X in one box: Check, Money Order, or Bill Me."

"I see. If I never pony up, they bill me and billmie."

"You got it. Now, how would you like to rent a room for roughly thirty bucks a month?"

"We can start there and raise it when I decide what craft I'm going to get into for a living. I imagine I'll have use for some of the back hallway, too, for work space."

"Unless," interjected Big Sylvia," you take in auto body work.

Sue decided to have a look at the crafts scene in Westwood. After dressing herself and gassing up William Randolph, she stopped at MacDonald's for a Big Mac and fries for the first time since accepting Venice vegetarianism to prepare herself for her venture into the world of commerce.

From the condition of Westwood Boulevard it was obvious the first show was out. She sneaked into town by the back way she remembered from her graduate school days and headed for her secret free parking space where she used to put The Bathing Machine, an old Nash almost as large as William. Amazingly, it was there as usual and fit William like an old shoe.

Down the street from the VD she found the craft fair in its sales alcove, packed, brightly lit and smelling of money. Stepping inside, she was caught up in the stream of the crowd, slowly swirling past each table with enough time to let her digest every detail of both crafts and craftspeople. It took forty minutes to make the circuit.

Sue kept coming back to watch the action around a young and portly woman named Jeanie, whose product was so simple it was staggering: strings of beads. The velocity of money over the table, and the size of Jeanie's purse brought Sue back at closing time.

"If I help you pack up, will you spill some trade secrets?"

Sue could not believe her own forwardness. All guilt vanished with Jeanie's answer: "In fact I'd appreciate your help, honey. On a night like this it's hard to get out of here without getting ripped off. As for trade secrets, not much to this. I sell a lot because I actually do a lot of my work right here, out in the open, so everyone can see what I'm doing."

Under Jeanie's direction Sue filled boxes, taking this opportunity to examine the details of Jeanie's work, and packed them into one very top-heavy grocery cart. This uncertain arrangement they perched on the curbside in Sue's charge while Jeanie whipped around the corner to the Safeway parking lot for her VW van. After the van was packed Jeanie got into the driver's seat, but Sue just stood there.

"Well, are you coming along or aren't you?" Jeanie laughed. In another ten minutes they were in a booth at Norm's all night restaurant over on Pico, sopping up a breakfast of wet eggs and toast, while Sue learned all about the resources of her new trade.

"I don't get it," Sue confessed. "Why would you share all this with me, when you know I'm going to be doing business at the alcove?"

"That's just the point, honey. With two of us selling beads, more people will figure they are OK to buy. My business will probably go up a good ten percent, which is about as much as I can produce without hiring someone, and that would be asking for trouble."

With her head full and her creative juices pumping, she headed for the beach with the windows open and a Carol King tape playing. She parked on the end of the Peninsula across from the Marina with its petite point of boats' lights in the midnight darkness. She opened the corpse door to let in the salt vapor from the waves on the rocks. By the light of the Coleman lantern she settled down to record her observations and ideas while they were still fresh and growing in her mind's eye.

When she awoke at dawn the lamp was out of oil. Beside it was a page obviously written by Sue herself. Amazingly enough, it was legible, although she had no recollection of writing it. She straightened out the wrinkles and creases in the paper and squinted to read the message:

You can't make a living doing women's work, so stay away from thread and string as a crafts medium.

Price tag is five times cost of materials, so don't work in any cheap materials.

People think they like something different. What they actually buy is close to current styles.

In an economic recession people will still buy, but prefer luxury items whose raw materials are recoverable and have intrinsic value, i.e., silver jewelry with semi-precious stones. *Question:* Where is the gold? No one is selling any gold.

Men buy expensive things for themselves sooner than for someone else. They are not wearing much jewelry. *Objective:* Design expensive men's jewelry. Contemplate gold.

The dominating style of jewelry is Hopi and Zuni tradition. The rings are the most popular, because the bracelets and necklaces are too large and heavy to wear to work.

Bead-stringing is very big.

What she read had the impact of 'writing on the wall', an exercise in Zen capitalism, a merger whose time had come, in Sue's mind at least.

What she needed was seclusion, a scarce commodity if you were living in everyone's laps the way people did in Venice. If Gary and Karen and Sylvia were at the house it was too late for a quiet, lazy Sunday morning there. She opened all of William's windows, closed all his drapes and drove him into the shade of the City parking lot by the sand at Venice Beach. Stripped to cut-offs and tank top, she alternatively racked up z's and pondered in seclusion. By eight-thirty Monday morning she was up and on the road to downtown L.A.—and home by noon with a one-foot package as big around as your thumb.

There in the living room were Gary, Karen and Big Sylvia. "Where have you been, and what are you up to? We haven't seen too much of you since last week," said Karen, more than slightly embarrassed.

"Right," said Sue. "And I've been to the Jewelry Mart Downtown, pricing beads of turquoise, coral, lapis, garnets, pearls and other semi-precious stones."

Gary shook his head. "Much too expensive."

"Right," said Sue. "Joking to myself I figured that, at the price of the expensive beads, I might just as well be stringing sterling silver."

"That's a really novel idea!" said Gary.

"There are no silver beads to speak of, so I priced silver in a form I might be able to make beads out of."

At that point Sue opened her thin package and rolled out a dozen one-foot lengths of silver tubing in several diameters.

"Oh, how beautiful!" exclaimed Sylvia.

Gary only smiled and chuckled.

"Everyone thinks silver is very expensive. Actually, the small-diameter stuff is only a buck a foot. Even the fat tube is only a tenth the price of semi-precious beads. I can make strings of mostly silver beads with a few stones for color, and charge the same price as if the strand were all turquoise. People will think they are getting the world's biggest bargain."

"Christ!" said Karen. "I think this could be better than selling dope!"

"What I like is how well the idea goes with Indian jewelry," said Gary. "It's a natural!"

"Now," said Sue, "all I have to do is learn to cut up the tubing into bead lengths."

You can't saw silver tubing into pieces and have decent silver beads. The cut edges are sharp, and are very irritating to your neck. The larger diameter beads tend to flop around on the string, and are not at all attractive. Once Sue got involved with this problem she stuck with it until a week later when she emerged from her confinement with a bunch of nicely-shaped beads and a production secret.

After two weeks' hard work she had enough necklaces to fill Karen's card table which she took to Westwood with a chair to sit on and a good flood light to display her product. Everyone was delighted to see something new for sale. The other bead stringers wanted to know where to buy her nice silver beads, or better yet how to make them, but Sue kept her trade secret to herself.

For the first time in weeks she slept in her jeans, but with green-backs stuffed safely in the pockets.

In the morning she indulged the delicious ritual of organizing her money. First she smoothed the blanket on her bed and emptied the wads and rolls of green-backs from the pockets of her jeans, shirt and jacket. Then she straightened each bill so it lay flat in the pile of bills of like denomination, and stashed her treasury in a hole at the back of her closet.

"What we need," she said to Toots, "is a bank account."

"Now," Karen ordered as she scooped up the dirty dishes, "you have just time enough for a fast bath and a change of threads. We're going over to see Katherine and Cherry."

"You mean I'm finally going to meet the famous Cherry?"

"I thought this would be a good chance for Cherry to do your numerology, and to check out the crazy tarot everyone has been getting for you. I've got business with Katherine. She needs help in her sign painting business—someone light enough not to fall off the ladder while she holds it up."

"It sounds like you are about to achieve your manifest destiny. Could this be a permanent thing?"

"It could, for about two days a week. Katherine works a lot in the evenings in her studio, and not later than noon during the day..."

"...so it won't disturb your Venice beach-bunny routine at all."

"...and I can go into L.A. on nights when Sylvia has a gig."

The route to Katherine and Cherry's was along the old way people went to Pacific Ocean Park—down Olympic Boulevard—a pre-freeway rushing headlong from the top at Lincoln Boulevard, under art deco overpasses arranged in stairsteps, past turnoffs to slower streets. Their two-story house was at the top-most overpass with a stunning view of Santa Monica's crisp pastels and twenty-four-karat waves.

Karen's timid knock at the heavy white door was answered immediately by two tall, thin women with lots of shining black hair, milk-white skin and chocolate eyes, decked out in overalls, starched white shirts and glasses with corrective lenses. They were both prospering, fine artists, but in most other respects they were opposites. Where Cherry's hair was decisively straight and carefully combed, Katherine's was coiled and springy like Franz Lizt's, with ringlets cascading at will. Where Katherine wore lace-up brown boots for hard work, Cherry slipped into Japanese rubber sandals.

"Now we can pour the Lapsang Suchong." Katherine said in a voice with the sand-and-gravel quality of a really blessed soprano. She led the way to a heavy hardwood country dining table painted last year with white enamel now streaked with the same bright latex as the blobs on her grey overalls, and on the two story mural in the atrium.

As soon as they had gulped their tea Karen and Katherine went off to do their business, and it was time for Cherry to

57

spread the cards for Sue. She tied back her waist-length straight hair, fussed for a while, spread the cards again, and finally announced, "There it is, every time, just like both Karen and Yaz predicted. Death and travel, money and sex. The future looks bright indeed."

"Hmm," Sue mumbled. "You know, Cherry, if I believed any of this stuff I'd be terrified about now. Recently I've been seeing a lot of Interstate Highway 1-5, I spent a fantastic weekend in the sack with a new lover, and my new jewelry business exceeds all of my hopes. Can death be far behind?" There! She had said it!

"I see your apprehension, but try not to worry. Death could apply to someone close to you rather than directly to you."

"Is that supposed to soothe my anxiety?" asked Sue. "I guess I'll just relax and enjoy my good fortune."

"What's that pendant I see around your neck?"

"The moon and star? It's made from a design I saw in one of Karen's magazines."

"That's the moon and Venus in conjunction, very powerful magic. The occultists would be interested in buying them, I think."

"The occult market—great. Can you turn me on to any other important signs?"

"Sure," Cherry said, and got out a few books and magazines.

"Try showing your work to Oak Woman at the Feminist Wicca, down on south Lincoln. I'm betting she can sell them as fast as you can make them. You know," she said after a pensive pause, "I admire artists like you and Katherine who manage to live by your work."

"I was under the impression you guys do pretty well."

"Oh, I sell something every so often at a good price through the local galleries, which is good for prestige. But Katherine keeps the cash coming in week after week." She refreshed Sue's cup and continued. "I spend most of my time at the new women's center teaching assertiveness and karate. Why don't you come down some time?"

Sue blew into her tea. "Thanks a lot, Cherry. Could karate combat that death threat in my tarot?"

"It couldn't hurt."

58

Chapter 8

Sue heard Danny Mae over the phone croaking, "I've got Nola and Thea, and we're discussing your financial condition. So come on over, OK?"

Once your car is parked on Sunday in Venice, you don't dare move it unless you're ready to leave town. Since Sue had come to stay, she left the hearse parked in front of her house and hoofed on over to Linnie Canal with Toots beside her.

The back yard was set for the meeting. Nola in her bare skin was filling the wading pool while Thea, with her wild mop of curly hair and wearing only her two pounds of silver chains and bracelets, sat in it and savored every drop of water. Nola pointed to a second vessel, another tub already full and waiting. "Get naked and get down so we can start this thing," Nola commanded.

"Now," said Danny, as chairman (or tubwoman) of the event. "We think you should apply for Disability Insurance."

Sue began laughing as she finished stripping and settled into the cool water. "Does this meeting involve disabling me? Where are you going to start? At the knees? I'm not disabled, Danny. Whatever makes you guys think I could ever get Disability?"

"We all get it," Nola confessed.

"Sure," Thea assured her, and continued with words that sputtered out like machine-gun bullets. "I understand you've got narcolepsy. Of all the people I know who are drawing Disability, you're the only one who deserves it."

"For twenty years you paid into that fund. You deserve to draw out of it." Danny's argument came the closest to making sense.

"Assuming for the moment that I decide to go along with this obvious fraud, what would I have to do to get it?"

"Very simple," said Danny. "There's a forty-page application form on the kitchen table. Fill it out, and call the phone number at the top of page one. He's the State's psychiatrist. Make an appointment to see him."

"See him?" Sue's eyebrows rose up to her hairline. "He'll take one good look at me and pronounce me the healthiest person on the block!"

"That's what I'm here for," said Thea.

Nola added, "Thea's a rock singer, and also acts in movies, which is why we need her help today, before she goes to Seattle on tour with the show."

Danny assumed her coaching mode. "The Disability people think you must be crazy, so Thea is going to teach you how to be a nut."

"You guys aren't going to give me a minute's peace until I go through with this, are you?"

"How did you guess?" Nola chortled.

"OK. As long as you are going to all this trouble, the least I can do is give it the old college try. So, Thea, let's get down to the acting lessons."

"So," began Thea, pleased that her professional talents were once more to be useful to someone besides herself. "We'll do what we actors call 'method' acting which always begins with motivation. In this little show you are psychotic, out of touch with reality, out of touch with everything and everyone around you. Never speak unless you are spoken to. Do not respond until the question is repeated. If you are forced to speak immediately, answer some other question instead. In other words, change the subject completely. Do not recognize the existence of anyone. Avoid eye contact. Let your gaze wander and drift to the floor. You can even get up and wander around every so often. Have you got all that?"

"Probably not," said Sue overwhelmed.

"You will, after a little role playing. Pretend I'm the doctor...."

After a short session of directed role-playing, Sue was performing admirably as a psychotic, and the Committee pronounced her ready for her debut.

Danny alone disagreed. "I don't know, gang. Sue has a face like an open-face sandwich: Everything inside is right on the surface. She won't be able to tell a lie, not a very big one anyway."

"What do you think? Are you going to be able to do this?" asked Nola. Sue shrugged inconclusively. For a smart woman, Sue could on occasion be something of a dumb bunny, you might even say, "asleep at the switch." Her particular disorder arose not from any lack of gray matter but from a lack of guile.

Thea shook her mop of curly hair. "I can show Sue the moves all right, but the nerve will take a whole lot longer than I have before my plane leaves for Seattle."

"I think," Nola suggested, "we should try her out on a little petty thievery before sending her in for the big prize."

"Impossible," Sue muttered, "impossible."

"Come on. Let's go find Karen. She and I will teach you how to rip off." With an arm around her, Nola led her off to Rialto Street.

The Three Musketeers, Nola, Karen, and Sue, stood in front of the drug store, where the main activity was dealing out drugs at the prescription of the doctor upstairs. "Is this a good place, or is this a good place!" said Karen.

"Great! These guys are so busy handing out free dope they won't even care you are here." Nola shifted to the other foot and continued. "What you do is, you mill around a little, and then clip one of their ball-point pens into your shirt pocket. Then you mill around a little more, shrug, and leave. Got it?"

"I guess," Sue said, screwing up her courage and opening the door. As soon as the assigned item was in her hands, her entire bearing changed from Venice casual to the resigned slump of guilt and sin. She left empty-handed. Clearly, a life of petty crime was out of the question.

Nevertheless, Sue decided to go through with the Disability scam. She was twenty minutes early to her appointment with Dr. Thurber, time enough for a review of the tactics which the

Committee assured her would get her a minimal stipend from State Disability. Unfortunately, the entry to his office was through a fashionable art gallery, folk-art and imports shop in Westwood. She dawdled from one glass case to the next until time was nearly gone, and she entered the office on the run, in a photo finish with the clock. 'Tactics' was the farthest thing from her mind.

"Good afternoon," said Dr. Thurber with a certain acerbic good humor. "Nice to see you."

"Considering the obstacles in the gallery downstairs, are you ever on time to work, and are there days you never completely arrive?" asked Sue. Inspecting the artistic decor of the office she continued, "And do you have trouble keeping a cash balance in your bank account?"

Dr. Thurber laughed. "My smart Korean wife keeps cash out of my pocket by packing my lunch and gives me a credit card good only for gas; otherwise I'd be grossly undernourished and reduced to traveling on a Rapid Transit pass."

"I brought my paper work from Disability," said Sue, handing over the fourty-page questionnaire. "I'm very good at paper work."

"Hmm. Yes, you certainly are. Your writing gets a little wiggly once in a while, though. Narcolepsy, you say."

"Yes. A pain in the ass. Somehow employers resented it when I fell asleep on the job and drooled all over my computer programs, or worse yet all over the computer. I have to warn people during a job interview, but that means they don't want to hire me at all."

"You know, I think that's your problem right there. Don't tell them before you're hired, then catch narcolepsy the first week on the job."

Sue shook her head is despair. "Everyone tells me I should tell more lies. Dr. Thurber, I have such a hard time telling lies, especially while I'm nodding off during the interview."

"Yes, I see. Maybe it's best not to try subterfuge after all. It doesn't suit your personality. I think it's Nixon, not narcolepsy that's keeping you out of work." He found a report form in his desk, filled it out and wrote a note on Sue's paper work. "Now go out there and give 'em all hell."

Sue strolled around Westwood for a couple of hours looking for new ideas in the current jewelry fashions. At last it was time to set up her table in the sales alcove. Business was at least as good as it had been the previous week. As she added one week's money to the other's in her wallet, she made plans for a savings account with a credit card machine so she could accept sales on credit.

After pack-up time at midnight she showed up at Nola's end of the bar at the Bacchanal, tired but pleased with herself, and in the market for a real drink. When Nola saw her she came running over. "So how did it go at the shrink?" she asked.

"After all the trouble you guys went to, with the acting lessons and all, I just couldn't go through with it. I played it straight. So I flunked. I came up sane."

Nola looked really disgusted. "What the hell was the matter with you? You knew exactly what to do."

"Look at it this way," Sue explained. "If I had put on the crazy act, he might have written down crazy on the report. He's a professional, Nola. I would then have had to face the possibility that I am really a nut case. Instead, he wrote ineligible, so I can safely assume I'm as sane as the next person. The way things go these days, that means something to me."

Nola thought a few moments, and then nodded assent. "So are you ready for a drink?" she asked.

Sue simply smiled and said "Make it Scotch-rocks."

"Since when did you start drinking?" asked Nola, amazed.

"Since I got something to celebrate." When Nola set the drink down, Sue handed her a fat wallet and said, "I just want you to go into the corner and count what's in here."

"Jesus Christ, Sue! There's fifteen-hundred dollars here!"

"Tax-free, if I don't tell the revenuers. I'll be doing this every two weeks as long as this crazy jewelry fad lasts."

"Are you sure what you're doing is legal?"

"Sure." Sue fished around under the bar and came up with a card-full of necklaces. "Look these over and pick out a present for yourself."

Who could tell whether Nola was more pleased or puzzled. "A

present? For me? Really? Why would anyone give me a present?"

"Because I like you, dummy. If you don't understand that, let's just chalk it up to advertising."

Nola's eyes lit up like birthday candles. "Oooh, they're all so pretty I can't stand it!" Nola's choice was a nice necklace featuring lapis and red coral, which Sue knew all along she would choose. No matter what you're creating, it comes out better if you have someone you like in mind.

"What I like about you," said Nola, "is that you work for your money, and you have good eye contact. I can't stand anyone I have to take care of all the time." She leaned across the bar to refresh Sue's drink and whispered, "Would you mind staying around after closing? Thea's show is on the road, so a certain element around here will come around asking me to do things I wouldn't ordinarily do. Be my body guard so I can get out of here without a big scene."

Sue nodded. When last call for drinks came, she took the easy jobs, picking up the empties, cleaning ash trays, wiping off the table tops, returning chairs to where they belonged. Finally the lights came on. Time to haul cases of empties to the store room and load warm beer into the coolers for the next evening. Nola swept the floor pocketing the lost coins she saw. When the last drunk had been ushered out, she bolted the front door and turned out all lights except the one remaining Coors sign over the back bar. The two women parted outside the back door, waving goodnight in the cool night air.

Sue lit off William's engine and was letting it warm, when she detected the insistent odor of fresh Canoe cologne at her elbow. "Why don't you pull this wagon over next to my bike," said Nola, "and I'll take us to breakfast at Carolina Pines."

Nola kicked over the mag on her chopped Honda, and it began to hum. Then she patted the spot on the seat Sue was to share with her. "Wait here a second. I forgot to pick up my tips."

Nola left her there in the alley with the engine going. It was warming between her legs and the low, consistent rumble of the engine, well-tuned and sustained, admonished her that she truly did love Nola. As she sat there wondering what she ought to do about it, Nola herself climbed into the seat in front of Sue, gunned the engine and they took off with a rap.

The late hour notwithstanding, Carolina Pines was packed with Hollywood gay men and lesbians getting breakfast before going home from the bars. Sue and Nola settled into a booth near the back and tied into an eggy breakfast.

As they sat there with their coffee Nola whispered, "Don't look now, but that booth over there is full of Thea's cronies. Ten bucks says one of them will make a phone call." Sure enough, it happened. "Now," Nola continued, "the phone will ring." It did. "For me from Thea, from Seattle."

"From *Seattle?*"

Presently there came the sweetly nosy call from the counter, "For you, Nola."

Nola was gone long enough to hang up. "It was herself, the Mafia queen, checking up on me," Nola said with satisfaction.

They rolled quietly down Sunset Boulevard in the late-night hour. The neon signs still flashed as if someone was still watching and willing to be enticed. Cars moved all right, but without the timely urgency of an evening out. "Let's go home," said Nola.

"Home? To Thea's?" Sue dared to speculate.

"I've got the key to Thea's, down on Vine Street." Where else? Surely not Karen's place, and who had the sense to check into a motel?

Sue could only gasp at—what was it, good luck or a compelling fate beyond her control? She let her arms firm their hold around Nola, and immediately felt a strong arm hold them closer. Helpless, Sue abandoned herself to the luxury of complete trust.

At Thea's courtyard, all the lights were out everywhere. Nola killed the engine and they floated silently down the walkway and stopped at Thea's door. Nola opened the door, and while Sue held it she rolled the bike into the living room and onto the tarp put there to catch the oil and dirt.

The rituals of showers, grass, and candles prepared and enjoyed, the two sank into the cool white sheets. Nola turned off the radio and they lay close to one another willing to let the quiet carry them the rest of the way.

Then Sue heard it, the sounds and squeaks and groans of

this unfamiliar house. All of their well-intentioned plans dissolved in fear.

"Damn!" exclaimed Nola. "My brain knows it's not Thea. She's way up in Seattle. But nothing tells my bones not to be afraid she might come blasting through that door ready to draw blood." Nola squeezed Sue's small hand in her large one. They looked into each other's sky-blue eyes. "How do you like your breakfast coffee?" Nola wanted to know.

"Hot, and in bed."

"You got it."

Finally they laughed at this ill-fated affair fallen apart for lack of nerve.

Chapter 9

Sue got home in the morning and washed up the last night's dishes while waiting a visit from Sapho arranged by Nola. At last there came the click of a woman's boots on the stairs and a business-like knock. As soon Sue opened the door she heard, "You must be Sue. I'm Sapho, Nola's sister."

"Yes," Sue whispered, "I see you are." Except for her wild black hair where Nola's was blonde, flashing black eyes where Nola's were soft and blue, and height, two inches short of Nola's six feet, Sapho could have been Nola's twin. Sue finally had regained her composure. "Come on in."

As Sapho walked to the mohair chair and assumed position there, Sue got a good look at her trim and healthy shape beneath her antique, filmy, 1930's dress, and decided she was probably heterosexual. It was too late. Sue had already fallen in love at first sight.

"I must say, you come well recommended," said Sapho to the blushing Sue. "I need some help from you and William Randolph, and I'm willing to pay for it, but not much, because this movie has a minuscule budget. I'm a film student at UCLA, and I'm ready to shoot my Master's film, an insane work about half an hour long." She lit a Sherman, took a long drag and continued. "I expect to finish within a week. We had better. Dana, one of the principals, will probably overdose on heroin soon after that. I need a strong vehicle to haul the equipment around, and a strong back to help load, unload and set it up."

"Count me in," said Sue as soon as she could get a word in edgewise.

"That was easy!"

"Have you ever known anyone in Venice to turn down the opportunity to work on any picture on any basis?"

"N-n-o," Sapho said. "I guess we all dream with the same parts of the brain out here. For as long as I can remember, it was carnival time when the equipment vans and food wagons came to town. And then, all the beautiful people! I would have given anything to be a part of it all. That's how I got my cast, incidentally. I watch people a lot. When I see interesting personalities who look like they dream of stardom, I ask if they want to be in my crazy student movie. No one has refused. What do you say? Could you start working Monday morning?"

Could she lay down her very life for Sapho? Could she embark on a week-long come-on? "As easy as not," Sue said, with the definite feeling she had been had, but enjoying the feeling of anticipation.

"All right!" exclaimed Sapho. "We are all going to spend Sunday together at my place on Sherman Canal, to turn on and get acquainted." Sunday began with eleven o'clock brunch: slabs of cheese cake, tumblers of fresh orange juice, Mexican coffee and the drug of your choice. Besides Sapho there were her younger brother Dean (sound technician), Nigel (talented cameraman and father of Sapho's four-year-old son Peter) and the principal actors, Jimmy and Dana whom Sapho had picked up on Ocean Front Walk. Jimmy and Dana, long-time friends, were waiting around for Jimmy's female hormone shots and psychotherapy to be finished so he could undergo a sex-change operation. Around these facts Sapho created the following story for the picture:

Dana had been subsisting as a prostitute, but had gotten too sick with bronchitis to be hanging around street corners. Jimmy found a bigger place to live at the same price as he had been paying for a hole-in-the-wall, so Dana could move in and have a place to keep warm.

Jimmy, now half man, half woman, was too weird to be employable in any usual business. No restaurant or store wanted a clerk of indefinable sex. He tried going back to his usual trade as a male prostitute, but with his new tits and fat buns he was no good at that either.

Dressed as a woman, Jimmy was nearly credible at a distance. The boys combined their talents. While Jimmy displayed himself in their apartment window, Dana pimped for him from the front porch, collecting the money before the disgusted customer's discovery, that Jimmy was not a woman, sent him running out of the place. With this ploy and Jimmy's welfare check, they hoped to survive until time for surgery.

That piece of intrigue plus a few associated incidents constituted the meager plot of the picture.

Production began on Monday morning. In order to find a realistically run-down 'location' in which to shoot most of the picture, Sapho gave Jimmy and Dana one hundred dollars and sent them out to rent an apartment for themselves to live in for the month. She was confident that hundred wouldn't buy much for that questionable duo, but she had no idea how run-down "rundown" was. When she walked onto the set for the first time she turned to Sue, her right hand, and said, "We're going to have to clean this place up a little. Otherwise, the critics will say we 'over-dressed' the scene."

Although the story was simple, there was funny-business to watch and a wide variety of locations, from a bar to a shoe store to a walk down one full mile of Hollywood Boulevard. People in Hollywood are amazing. They never ruin your take by looking into the camera.

Every change of scene meant back-breaking labor. Dean and Nigel and Sue wrestled the cases of equipment in and out of the hearse, and placed the lights and mikes. When it came time to shoot, Nigel ran the camera, Dean ran the sound recorder and Sue held the mike out of the picture. Sapho directed, in her own inimitable fashion.

Filming a scene began with getting the actors all together, in costume, on the readied set. Sapho explained what the scene was to convey, and roughly described the action surrounding it. Then they ran through it with the dialogue improvised by the actors as they went along. After the run-through, Sapho had a few new ideas, as did the actors and even the rest of the crew.

The actors wrote notes to themselves on tablecloths, magazines, the backs of their hands, any place convenient to remind themselves of the sequence of events and dialogue. After three or four of these revisionary rehearsals the scene was smooth enough for filming. The camera rolled, the recorder ran, action went to film with heightened life under the tension of filming.

As often as not something went wrong and the scene had to be shot again. Amazingly, about half the takes were printable and survived editing for the final version of the film, a record few directors can equal. Occasionally some unforeseen circumstances disrupted the take and were interesting enough to become a part of the movie. For example:

The elements of the plot were simple. The rent was long overdue. Jimmy decided to pay it with his Welfare money, which he had been saving for his hormone shots, and sent Dana down to the landlady with the cash. The scene was dinner time. Dana confessed that, instead of paying the rent, he bought dope to cheer Jimmy, who seemed depressed (because of hormone imbalance, obviously).

In the ensuing argument, one of them accidentally tipped over the candle, which Jimmy had lit for romantic atmosphere. The curtains caught fire, and they played the rest of the scene while slapping down the fire and dousing it with orange juice. The scene ended as originally intended: While the two men kissed and made up, two strangers sneaked in, stole the dope, and ran off into the night.

An unforeseen circumstance nearly cancelled the whole picture. As the scene opened, Dana and Don, one of the minor characters for whom Dana had a flashing affection, were naked in the walk-in closet, dressing to go to a party at Mick Jagger's. The scene didn't further the plot, it only gave Dana a chance to dress up and clown around. Then it happened: Dana had his back to Don and was putting on his pants, allowing Don and the audience to have an open, spread view of his rear.

"Holy cow! What's the matter with your bung hole?" shouted Don.

"Oh, it's nothing to worry about. The doctor says it's only a case of secondary syphilis."

"*Syphilis!* Lemme outta here!" Don grabbed his clothes and ran out naked into the hallway. He never came back, but he was in the picture. The rest of the film company worried about their own states of health. Not that anyone had done up with Dana, but there had been a lot of clothing exchanged. So they all took a long lunch and got tested. All were negative including Jimmy and Dana, but there had been a few tense moments.

Sapho's method of writing and directing demanded a will of iron and the leadership qualities of a drill sergeant. Her control over her flaky little filming company bore up admirably until day number two. After lunch break, her 1958 Mercedes was gone from its parking place. Nigel and Dean were nowhere to be seen.

While waiting for the men to come back, Sapho sat beside Sue in the hearse as they ate a second order of burgers and Cokes. Probably because Sue was an outsider to the family, Sapho confided, "My life would be a whole lot simpler if only I didn't love Nigel, and if he weren't such a damn fine camera-man. I could fire him right now, and would never again have to worry about him o.d.-ing some place. He came so close to death last month. I came home and found Peter's daddy on the bed, as still as death. He was so low, I couldn't find a pulse, and I couldn't see any breathing at all. But he wasn't blue, so I went to work on him and saved him again. Someday, I'll be five minutes too late, and Peter won't have a daddy any more."

About three o'clock the men were back. They had connected with a dealer in downers, and stumbled onto the set entirely incapable of working and intent only on skipping out for the day.

"Sue, you can run the recorder," Sapho said, with more hope than conviction.

"I think so," said Sue. "I've been watching Dean. I under-stand the recorder, and I think I know the drill for the take."

"Super. The one thing you don't know is that you have as much power to 'cut' as anyone else. Pay attention to things like camera noise, street noises. They can ruin a take. OK?"

Sapho ran the camera, and that's the way they finished the day. Late in the afternoon Nigel and Dean finally showed up at the set, sobered, with Dean's car. Dean drove off with Dana.

Sapho was waiting for Nigel on the set with Jimmy and Sue to keep her company. Pissed at being treated like an infant, Nigel fucked the landlady. For a last hurrah he left in a blur of

71

Mercedes chrome with Jimmy seated next to him.

"Damn Nigel!" Sapho said. "Now what do I do about a jab like that?" Answering her own question, she gave Sue a deliberately smoky look which demanded an immediate answer.

"You heterosexual women drive me crazy," said Sue, just loud enough to be overheard and soft enough to be inviting.

Sapho gave her a nice kiss by the ear, and whispered, "How about a guided tour of your studio tonight?"

"Any time after supper."

Sue looked up from her work bench to see Sapho tip-toe up the stairs barefoot with her boots in hand. Sapho leaned on the studio door until it shut tight. With her heart in her mouth Sue asked, "How did you get away from—"

"Nigel has passed out. Dean is in the Venice Division jail for driving under the influence. Peter is at Mom's with Nola—"

"Nola!" gasped Sue. "How am I going to explain this to her?"

"She'll never hear it from me. What about Karen in there?"

"So long as I'm not with Nola, Karen can keep any secret. Besides," Sue giggled, "Karen is nearly deaf in one ear."

"Then what are we waiting for?"

For 'making love' you need love at the very least, trust, tenderness and sexual attraction. For 'good old orgasms' you need only lust, but a dollop of anger and stamina couldn't hurt. Whatever they did there on Sue's narrow cot was all of those, beginning as revenge against people not present, and finishing with two women who cared for each other. There's nothing like sex for getting acquainted.

All the next day Sue found herself thinking more often than usual about sweet Yazmina whose speech center was connected to her genitalia, thinking maybe she was in love with that crazy woman. And what about Sapho the human carnival? To know her was to lust. For Sue, whose luck was not always so good, all of this was nearly enough to make her trust the tarot cards.

At week's end they watched all the rushes at once. It was funny, it was honest, it was flaky, it was wonderful, and it was featured at Filmex.

When at last the filming was finished and the equipment

hauled one last time (back to the Department at UCLA), it was time for everyone to become unglued, each in whatever way he or she had been stressed during the week of the shoot. Close to physical as well as emotional collapse, Sue headed for the therapy of sun and sand. How could she have guessed that, in her absence, local affairs had gone to hell in a hand-basket?

Sue spread out the blanket and squinted southward to the Pavilion while Karen's more accustomed eye combed the beach north to the rocks of Santa Monica. "Nowhere," pronounced Karen as she emptied the sand out of her tiny tennies and settled her micro-surfer frame on the soft cotton. "And no one has seen any of them all day."

"I'm really worried. What could keep all of Highland House off the beach all at once? Arson? Mass murder? A drug bust?" Count on Sue for something comforting.

"We would have heard something by now. It's got to be worse, much worse."

Sue stood, pulled on her T-shirt and rubber sandals. "Well I'm going to look for them. Everyone from Highland House is missing, and I can't just sit here in the sand thinking the worst." She tossed Karen's tennies at her feet. "Come on. If they're in the lock-up, we still have an hour to get bail money before the bank slams shut."

With the blanket under her arm, Karen loped through the deep sand and stopped at the walkway to catch her breath and wait for Sue. "Can you believe it? Both of us wastrels with enough legit money in the bank to cover bail for a whole household?"

"We haven't seen the bill yet. But it does seem ironic." After a vigorous walk over to the Canals they stepped over the picket fence, listening for some signs of life emanating from Highland House. Sue cocked first her left, then her right ear. "All I hear is a kind of low, miserable...moaning? Can it be moaning?"

"You couldn't prove it by me. I've been half deaf since the early days of rock and roll." Karen knocked on the front door, which swung open by its self with an unearthly grating squeak. "Jesus! All we need now is some zombie with electrodes in his neck!"

"Oof," came a low, rasping groan which could conceivably have been sexual under other circumstances. "Is that you, Little Karen?" the voice asked.

"Me and Sue. Are you OK, Danny Mae?"

"Shit! Are you guys dead, too? There's this black hole where I used to have center-vision. It's death waiting to expand and suck us all in!"

Sue squatted and peeled back Danny's eyelids for a clinical look. "You look alive to me. Hang onto the chair leg there while we check on the rest of the house."

"See about Juice," Danny asked. "Tough, but maybe can't handle this one."

Evelyn and Flor were on the sleeping bag in the garden shack, squeaking in misery and hiding their heads. Charles was spread-eagled on the kitchen floor, hanging from the cracks between the floor boards. Juice was quiet and feeling safe, wrapped in a blanket under the bed in Danny's room. Sue kissed her sweaty little cheek and made sure she smiled a bit before reporting back to Danny.

"Everyone's alive, and looks about like you," said Karen. "What the fuck is going on here, Danny?"

"Bad trip. We did something new and orange and deadly. Thank god we only had half a pill apiece. Testing the dope before we sell it." Danny opened her hand to show a plastic bag with a plethora of orange hell.

Karen grabbed it and headed for the phone. "Thank heaven you didn't sell any! I'm calling the KMET dope hotline so they can warn everyone."

After feeding the dogs and cats, Sue found paper and a Crayola to make a sign for the front door: "Please do not disturb the occupants until Monday noon."

Chapter 10

While her eyes and skin adjusted to the dark and chilly ambiance of the Club Bacchanal, Nola wiped the daytime dust from the tables and found all the stools that belonged to 'her' bar at the back of the place. Someone, probably the manager, had already carried the ice for both back and front bars, so she fussed a little longer over filling the cherry, olive and onion bowls to accommodate the heavy-drinking early crowd.

Happy hour drew its usual cadre of live-alones intent on quick intoxication in lieu of the comforts of home, and an early exit to pass out for the rest of the evening. Back at the pool tables the experts convened early for three hours of uninterrupted play before the crush of the weekend amateurs. The clink of ice cubes merged indistinguishably with the strike of the pool balls. The bar was open for business as usual.

The place shifted gears abruptly at nine o'clock. Nola lit the candles on each of her tables as she cleared away the trash and the empties. Then she primed the juke box with a handful of marked quarters and punched up enough of the good numbers to last until the band unpacked and plugged in. When the manager arrived to collect the cover charge, Nola shut the front doors, turned on the neons and assumed her position behind the bar, ready to face her public which began to collect at the rail.

Everyone in Los Angeles, from Venice to Hollywood and East L.A., loved Nola. And why not, that Amazon beauty with a heart of gold? For her part, Nola fell in love every three days, and anyway couldn't say no. Ordinarily she enjoyed the benefits of her bartender's office unless she wanted to preserve a bartender's neutrality. On those occasions one of her Venice pals became a buffer, seated at the end of the bar where Nola retreated to chat when the business slowed.

Nola reserved the buffer spot with its ash tray and tall orange juice just as the Venice crowd tumbled out of William Randolph and stormed into the bar. Tanned and scrubbed and smelling good, dressed for anything in their best tank tops, patched jeans and ragged sneakers, the beach bunnies took command of the Bacchanal with a promise of a rowdy and drunken evening.

"Sue! I've been looking for you," shouted Nola from the far end of the bar.

With her hands in her pockets Sue shuffled on over to the buffer spot and took a long pull on the straight orange juice. "I see you've been expecting me," she said. "Which one is it?"

"Half way down the bar. The dark hair. What is it about her I don't like?" asked Nola.

Sue took a long look. "Hmm. For one thing, it looks like someone else combed her hair. Ironed blouse? And new jeans? I'd say she has an adequate, regular income. I think she's slumming here at the Bacchanal."

"Maybe it's the regular income that interests me. There are too many I'd end up taking care of, and I have all the trouble I need with just myself. And she's pretty. She's been sitting there since seven o'clock."

"Maybe she's nice."

"She seems to be."

"Maybe you're just nervous because she obviously has a big thing for you."

For all her cool, Nola totally blushed. "Why don't you go cruise the new band leader for a while?"

The trip to the bandstand was worth while if you like scenery. For one brief moment Sue considered the possibility of falling in love with the new band leader, but decided that would be about as sensible as falling in love with Mount Rushmore or some other community resource.

After a brief encounter with a man and woman standing near the bandstand Sue headed back to the bar, stopping on the way to check on Danny over in a corner with a red-head. Karen was comfortably surrounded by Sylvia. Evelyn and Flor were wound around each other on the pretext of dancing.

Back at the buffer spot, Sue lit a cigarette and drank half of the fresh, icy juice Nola had waiting for her. "She's Jill, from the Valley," said Nola. "And she wants me to go to a party, Sunday in Orange County."

"Voila! You're going, I presume?"

"What am I going to tell Thea? If she finds out, I'm chopped liver," Nola groaned.

"I've never known you to check in with Thea or anyone else. If you want permission, you've got mine."

"I said I'd go, if I could bring my friends. You'll go, I hope, and I'll get Karen, too."

"Sure," Sue said. "By the way, do you know the man and woman over there to the right of the bandstand?"

"Never saw them before."

"They asked me to go home with them. Something about a load of cocaine." said Sue with a definitely puzzled look.

"Coke is very chic these days, if you've got the bucks. You might enjoy it's natural 'upper' qualities. Go along with them, if you dig three-ways."

"Is that what they're up to! I was wondering why a straight couple were hanging around a gay bar. I guess you can find anything you want somewhere in Hollywood. And no, I don't dig three-ways."

At closing time the Venusians piled into the hearse and either passed out or fell asleep to the soft late-night radio music over the stereo speakers in the back compartment. Body steam cooled in the jasmine air through the open windows as they cruised quietly and slowly westward on the Santa Monica Freeway toward the beach. At that late hour and on the empty road Sue owned the city.

Finally each passenger had been safely delivered to her home and Sue was driving slowly down Main Street. Behind her she saw a black-and-white police car without the hat-light or insignia lit, strictly against the rules during shift hours. With their vehicle thus de-commissioned, the two uniformed policemen inside were no more than working stiffs off duty and looking for action when they should have been heading for home.

Suspecting they might be following, she drove once around the Circle before heading off toward Rialto, and around two blocks extra before parking in front of Karen's place. The black-and-white parked right behind her.

She walked slowly around the hearse, checking all the doors, and then walked slowly and boldly over to the cop car. Her message was clear and sober. "If you don't leave immediately, I'm going inside to call a cop." Like that, they were gone.

Sunday the day of the party with Jill from the valley they drove William Randolph through rutted roads, finally parking in the shade beside the house in Westminster, at Orange County's heart if it had one. Sue apprehensively inspected the greying frame house with its drab, untended yards, the tall grasses gone to seed. Sue pontificated: "This town reminds me of the San Fernando Valley in about 1950: Culturally unpromising."

"I see a lot of men in there," said Nola, "and they don't look gay to me. What kind of a mess have I gotten us into?"

"Sue, are you sure you can get us out of here?" asked Karen.

"Sure. We keep going west and/or north."

She was about to do just that when the back door sprang open to emit Jill, as pressed and combed as she had been the other night at the bar. The beach bunnies relaxed as the familiar figure of Jill confirmed the existence of the place they had come to. "Can someone drive me downtown to connect for some cocaine?" They all looked at Sue, who simply nodded. "You two can go on in and introduce yourselves," the hostess said to Nola and Karen.

William Randolph swallowed Jill in the tuck-and-folded leather of the front seat. "Can you get to downtown?" she whispered from the depth of luxury.

"Sure," Sue promised. "We came that way. Just holler directions when we get near where we're going." The rutted dirt road turned quickly back to asphalt and then to the cracked and dusty slab street of a defunct grove-town with angle parking at the curb.

"Turn right at the next corner," Jill said, looking carefully at

78

each store and doorway. "Now pull over and I'll get out. Cruise around the block a few times and I'll meet you back here."

As she turned the corner Sue looked back just in time to see Jill's connection come out from a negligible space between a bar and a furniture store. Jill was waiting for her the next time around the block.

Once back home, Jill set up at a glass-topped coffee table where she cut out a line of white powder for each of the guests patiently queued up for it. Sue found Nola and Karen about half way to the head of the line, and let them have it:

"Just for once, you two, please indulge my paranoia. I just didn't like the way the buy went down. It didn't even happen inside a house, just out on the street in the middle of town. I think he was a complete stranger. Who knows what's in that package she got? We're used to dealing with Danny or someone else we know and trust, someone who will do a number or a line from the ki your piece came from, just to prove it's righteous stuff."

"You've been watching too much television. Come on, Karen. Let's get back in line here."

What else could Sue do but find a cola, roll a number, and sit off by herself, soul-searching while her friends worked up to the front of the line. Having had zero experience with cocaine, she watched for its effects on the guests. It was like Nola said, an upper, giving the party energy and good humor. Suddenly the picture changed completely. One by one, in the order in which they had snorted, the guests went crazy! Shouting and flailing, each turned inward, running aimlessly to escape something or other both frightening and malevolent. Soon it seemed to Sue she was the only sane person there.

Where were Nola and Karen? They might run into something, or possibly one of these paranoids would actually hurt one of them. Sue searched the house, upstairs and down. Outside! Over there by William Randolph! There they were, both slumped over the hood. Sue ran to them, gathered one under each arm and spoke softly, "From the way everyone looks, I think you have gotten into some bad L.S.D. on the back of speed. I don't know anything about bad acid trips, so I'll have to leave that

79

part to you. You've had acid before, so you know how to handle what's going on inside your head.

"I promise it will be over soon. And I promise not to let anyone or anything hurt you or bother you until you get back to reality." Nola nodded, relieved in her fright. Karen snuggled in closer, tearful and shaking. "Now we'll move ourselves into the back of the hearse so I can keep track of you," Sue continued.

In the comfort of the hearse soothed by the Joan Baez album and the physical closeness of their one sober friend, Nola and Karen were soon well enough to fall asleep. Three hours after they had left Venice they were back home again with a six pack of beer and a bag of burritos.

"Shazam," Shouted Karen.

Chapter 11

For several nights the light in the gardening shed behind Highland House had been dark and its bed roll cold. Flor had flown the coop, taken the bus back to East L.A. and her old trade of hustling the boys in the barrio. Poor Evelyn was beside herself. She took to sleeping at the foot of Danny's bed wrapped in a thin cotton blanket and crying her eyes out. "What am I going to do, Danny? I think I'm going to die or something," she wailed over and over.

What Danny did was drop some good acid and consider the situation. When the mushroom clouds cleared she had some answers. "The trouble with Flor is, she wants to get married. Without a wedding her fling with you was never consecrated, never real, and she was the same old whore as ever. Some people dream from early childhood of a large, noisy wedding with food and music and maybe even the police if everyone has as much fun as they should. Anything less, the deal falls apart from guilt."

"So what am I going to do, Danny?"

"Go find her and propose properly. And tell her my wedding present to her is a big Mexican wedding."

Sue liked what she saw in the mirror: A seersucker jacket with red and white stripes, crisp white pants, blinding white tennis shoes.

A voice sneaked in behind her. "What you need now is the yellow straw hat." It was Katherine, another client of the Venice Salvation Army Store, wearing white tux pants and carrying her gray and paint-splotched overalls.

"Good. The voice of good taste. We're having a garden wedding in a couple of weeks, did you know?"

"I did know. That's why I'm here, before the rush, but I guess you beat me to the good stuff. Flor must be very pleased."

"Not to mention Evelyn," said Sue. "She has been frantic for some way to tie Flor down, as impossible as that is to achieve in the lesbian world."

"You've really got to work at it," said Katherine philosophically. "By the way, did you hear we're pregnant?"

"Is that so? You or Cherry?"

"Cherry, naturally. We had a long talk, and decided what our arrangement needed was a kid, so she went and did it." Responding to the unasked question all over Sue's face Katherine continued, "With the husband of one of her friends from high school days. They were all three pretty close in days gone by."

"What's he like?"

"Well, he's handsome and smart, and a little too anxious to accommodate, if you ask me. But the job is done now."

"Congratulations, I think," offered Sue. "But to my old and jaded ears it sounds as hard to believe in as 'civilized' divorce. Nothing good ever came of that idea, either."

"Kimmey! You're in town?" Sue said into the phone.

"Yea. Couldn't stay away from the rays too long. I brought Yaz with me this time."

"Yaz! There went my blood pressure! Where are you?"

"We're apartment-sitting over the carousel."

"You mean the carousel with the wooden wild horses and mirrors and the calliope that plays popular songs? Over on Santa Monica Pier? And I'll bet you came in Patty's black Ferrari. That should keep her out of the soup for a while."

"Why don't you guys come over for dinner?" Kim said through the tin-horn din of the carousel down stairs playing *You Are My Sunshine*. "We'll phone out for pizza and Cokes."

"We're on the way. It will be just me and Karen. Sylvia is in the Valley getting the sound system set up for her new gig."

Sue and Karen got under way down Main Street just as the

82

police were changing shift, while the new replacements were still fresh and paranoid about anything as strange as a hearse on the streets. Inevitably a whirling red hat-light flooded Sue's rear mirror and a short blast on the siren pulled her over. The policeman walked once around the hearse, asked for identification and radioed L.A. Division for a make on the hearse and both women. Disappointed when he came up with no priors and no warrants, he put his head in the window and flashed his light around inside looking for liquor or marijuana or pills.

"We're as clean as a hound's tooth," Sue whispered to Karen.

"But if he doesn't find something to give us a ticket for, like an equipment failure, he'll be in trouble with his boss and the judge. Pray he finds something cheap to fix."

"Now watch this," said Sue. Just before the cop came around to the rear, she hit the brake pedal and held it. Immediately he wrote something short and came back to talk.

"Sorry I had to stop you ladies, but your left rear brake light doesn't work. Get it fixed and have a highway patrolman sign this citation, send it in and there's no fine or anything. Good evening, now."

As soon as it was safe they started laughing. "It's so easy, and cheap. Before I have it checked, I screw the bulb back in for a while."

Overloaded with adrenalin and anticipation, Sue's mind returned to thoughts of Yaz. "Look, old pal," said Sue. "Could you and Sylvia possibly stay in town tonight? I don't know how Yaz would react to a crowded apartment..."

"...and Sylvia is quite a crowd," Karen mused. "We were planning on it anyway. You're funny when you're in love."

"Take William Randolph, after dinner. Sylvia loves to play 'limousine'."

Soon they came to the Santa Monica pier, and dove down into the parking lot underneath. In the dusk, the surf and the tin carousel music, it felt like the finale to a Fellini movie. As they climbed the short flight of steps, the flash of mirrors and lights, the silent, galloping carousel horses frozen in action, all convinced Sue she must be asleep and dreaming. She stopped in her tracks, ready to crash out.

"Come on! Let's get out of here!" cried Karen. Sue shuddered, regained consciousness, and they went on to the apartment above. Kim and Yaz met them at the door with open arms and the smell of fresh pepperoni. Suddenly the unfamiliar became a carnival celebration for old friends.

The party soon reverted to general uneasiness, each person suffering for her own reasons. Yaz especially seemed distracted, uneasy, longing to be elsewhere. Hoping to amuse everyone and warm up the evening Sue dropped her load of juicy Venice gossip.

First, there was the news of Cherry's impending motherhood. "I think it's wonderful, Cherry going to have a baby," Karen said, as starry-eyed as anyone had ever seen her.

Kim chuckled. "She's a size large in her natural state. When she gets close to delivery, she'll be as big as the Queen Mary."

Karen looked from Sue to Kim and back again. "What do you mean 'delivery?' What do you mean, 'big?'"

"That's to be expected now that Cherry's pregnant, isn't it, Karen?" said Sue, somewhere between puzzled and indignant.

"Pregnant? Is Cherry pregnant?" Now Karen began to get upset.

"I told you she's going to have a baby," said Sue.

Karen rose from her chair, ready for battle. "Pregnant? How in hell did she get pregnant?"

"In the regular way, I presume," said Sue.

"But she's a lesbian!" said the devout Karen.

Kim stared from Karen back to Sue. "I wonder how far back in this process we have to go, to explain it to her?"

Karen folded her little arms and retreated into a general funk. "Well, I hope she hated it at least."

Then Sue dropped her second news flash. The up-coming wedding. Kim was hopeless. "How can Flor marry Evelyn? She loves me and I love her! What am I going to do about this, Sue?" Sue had nothing comforting to offer Kim's poor broken heart, but only let her cry and talk.

Yaz, who hadn't stopped fidgeting since the party began, leaped into the conversation. "I've got a little matter to take care of myself," she announced in a huff at an emotional distance enforced by searching for her sweater.

Sue got Kim's attention receiving only an uncomprehending shrug in return. She could only hand William's keys to Karen, "Could you please drop Yaz where she's going? Kim can run me home in the Ferrari later."

When the two others had left, Sue and Kim sat staring at each other surrounded by the whirl and clang from the steam organ in the carousel downstairs. "I wonder," said Sue, "Who's on Yaz's mind."

Kim shook her head in amazement. "Man, I don't know, but she sure was hot to trot! The way she came on to you that day at Maude's, and after your two-day shack-up, and as pleased as she was to be riding down here with me, I would have bet anything it was you on her mind."

"She keeps a secret pretty well." Feeling justified in complaining, Sue continued. "Here I am, randy as hell. I was ready to drag her into the bedroom there, and she pulls a disappearing act!"

The carousel wound itself up again and let go with another chorus of *You Are My Sunshine*. "Sometimes," Kim agonized, "I feel like a merry-go-round myself. Too bad you and I aren't lovers, Sue. That might solve the whole mess."

"That's just what you need, another woman to drive you crazy! For my part, I long ago learned not to fall in love with my therapist."

"What I need right now is a little therapy," Kim groaned, pouring a new beer into her glass, and looking hopefully at Sue.

"All right," Sue said. "We'll get more beer, and go to my place, away from that crazing carousel. I'll buy one of Karen's new lids, and we can get productively high."

"I like that plan," said Kim, smiling. In half an hour they were sitting on Karen's living room floor with beer and bong, propped against the lower bunk.

Sue had the questions all ready, hoping for good answers from Kim. "Well, you could begin by explaining a few mysteries. I'll grant you Flor is a nice girl, even on the pretty side, but what in the world is so appealing about her that you beat your brow and the pavement until you see her? And why is Patty so mad at you she's ready to kill? Maybe if you tried telling me, you could get yourself a little better organized."

"You really don't know?" asked Kim.

"If I knew, would I ask?" said Sue.

"OK. You could say Flor originally appealed to me because she's half Mexican; as if that could explain falling in love. Patty doesn't really know about how I feel about Flor. She just knows that in some ways she can't compete with my memories of Singer, and she's right."

Sue was completely amazed. "You mean the famous, one and only Singer?"

"You mean, you don't know about Singer?" said Kim surprised.

"It seems to me I heard something or other, but I seldom pay attention to gossip, and I figured if it was important, whatever it was, I'd hear from you."

"Amazing! You never asked. You're the only one who hasn't at one time or another hung around asking what she's really like. The answer is, she's the best; and just because you never pried into my personal affairs, I'll tell you the whole story, the one no one else really knows.

"I was really young, seventeen years old, and I had run away from home with no money, and without even a change of clothes. It started to rain, even before I got out of town, so I parked my motor cycle in front of the post office, the only open door in town, left open for mail drops on weekends, and warm inside. It was ten o'clock on Saturday night. I was huddled way at the back of the place, under a table, to dry off and sleep a little, but she saw me anyway, and came in and took me home with her. I had no idea who she was. To me, she was the beautiful rich lady in the Jaguar. I heard she sang or something. I'll never know what she saw in me, I was so wet and miserable and dirty. I guess it was her warm heart.

"Anyway, we were alone together for several days while it rained and rained. I had never been with a woman before, but she got through to me and we finally made love. Singer was and still is, the most wonderful thing that ever happened to me.

"She was going East on a big tour, and hired me to go along as her driver. One thing I do well is drive fast. Most of the time we traveled by train, though. She would go out and sing for all those thousands of people who loved her to death, and then come home to me, completely drained, needing to be filled up again. It was a strange kind of power I had, so frightening I was uncomfortable at times. We went all over the East and South, and Singer inspired everyone and worked on school desegregation, singing and marching and everything.

"Finally I couldn't keep her filled anymore. She needed several more people to do the job, and I just wasn't up to sharing, so I left."

After a long silence Kim went on. "I used to wonder, after I've already had the best the world has to offer, what was there left for me? What could I do with the rest of my life? There were times I just about offed myself. I suppose that's why I let Patty do what she does. And then I met Flor and had to admit there's nothing wrong with absolutely wonderful."

By then Sue was out of questions, Kim was out of answers, out of beer and out of it. After tucking Kim into the lower bunk Sue crashed in her own room and heard nothing until the clap of a woman's boots interfered with her morning's drowsing. She zipped up her cut-offs, dove into a T-shirt and, in order to let Kim sleep a bit longer, opened the door before the knock.

Standing on the doorstep in hand-made boots, tailored pants and Chinese shirt was a well-maintained young woman with coal-black hair, flawless skin and the smell of money. "You're Patty," ventured Sue. "If you promise to be quiet for a while, you and I can have some words in my studio." With the coffee pot and two cups they sat on the floor and talked in whispers with the door shut.

"I've come for Kim."

"How in hell did you find her?"

"Elementary, my dear Watson. I just looked around for my Ferrari."

"Shit! I could have put it in the alley."

"Don't burden yourself, Sue. I'd have found her by now in any case," said Patty. "Parking in the alley might have saved my front tires, though. There's a three-inch slice in the side of each one. So much for Venice!"

"I don't understand this. Tire slashing isn't Venice style at all. This neighborhood is barrio. You can sleep with your doors open, you can leave your car overnight with the keys in it. I have never heard of anyone having their tires slashed. Very strange."

"Strange to you maybe," said the indignant Patty. "but it happens every time I come to town. Can I use your phone? By now the Michellin agency in Santa Monica is open. What would I do without credit cards?"

Finally new tires were on the way, and Patty articulated her fondest wish. "Do you mind if I get off?"

Not quite understanding what this meant she said, "I guess not." Then Sue fully realized what she had agreed to, but it was too late to take it back.

Patty got her outfit out of her purse and opened it. In a flash she loaded the syringe from a pharmaceutical bottle with a clear fluid in it and a rubber diaphragm in the top. She had a modicum of class and sanitation after all. With the band around her upper arm she pumped her fist, waited until the right vein rose, and then slipped the needle between two marks in a growing track. She pushed the plunger, and when the glass was empty she released the band, waited for the rush and said, "Now go get Kim for me."

"First tell me one thing. Why does she let you do this to her?"

"Easy," said Patty. "She wants someone to take care of her. Don't we all? I wish she wouldn't come to town in that crate. She'll only get into a mess of trouble. Go get her please?"

With an ounce of encouragement Sue would have sent Patty bouncing down the back stairs, but figured that kind of action was Kim's business. Instead, she opened up the living room window, turned the radio to something soft and whispered to Kim. "The Wicked Witch of the North is here. You're not going to let her shoot you up, are you?"

Ashamed and resigned, Kim answered "How can I resist?"

Sue had to admit that Patty was no dumb bunny, but would she have the sense to get Kim out of town before Flor's wedding that very afternoon?

For weeks the word had been widely spread with telephone bells ringing out the news that Flor and Evelyn would marry. As the appointed hour approached the guests arrived by bus, by cars parked up and down the Venice Boulevard median, by bicycles chained to lamp posts and pilings, by barefoot along the sand. All paths converged at Allan's Market to buy a beverage to last until the reception. The parade progressed down the road, across the bridge, along the Linnie quay and over the picket fence at Highland House.

Gay and lesbian friends from beach, bars and ball games came decked out in the latest fashions appropriate to the life-style they lived. From North Hollywood and South Bay came the gainfully employed in crisp, new and pressed pants-suits and ruffled shirts. From East L.A. came flowered prints, shirts tucked into jeans, and an occasional dress. From Westside came the caftans, bare feet, and Nehru jackets.

The Salvation Army, Goodwill, and Sylvia's Rummage up on Lincoln had long ago sold out of good contemporary second-hand clothing. They responded to Venice' demand by breaking out their dusty collections of old classics from 1920 to 1950. Revived for the wedding were '30's high-top pants with three-inch cuffs worn with white dress shirt and suspenders, nets and laces revealing more than they covered, seersucker suits, white tuxedos, morning coats. To some of the more theatrical minds, a wedding suggested less a rite than a celebration, and they came in costumes appropriate to Mardi Gras.

Highland House, not notably endowed with greenery, was suddenly popping with flowers on wedding day. Guests from all over Venice and beyond picked the flowers of summer from their own back yards and tied them with string to the California chaparral in brief graftings to mystify your average horticulturist.

It was time. The music began. Jimmy, in black tux pants, polished shoes and bare sun-browned chest, entertained on his new electronic keyboard as the guests settled themselves on the cool grass. At a signal from Danny at the back door Jimmy began the processional, *The First Time Ever I Saw Your Face*, sung by Big Sylvia from the second story window.

Heading the procession was Danny, in white tank top and cut-offs just above a fresh ace bandage, hair golden from shampoo and drying in the rays, smelling of ozone and electricity. Following were the giddy principles—Evelyn, the All-American Girl, in blue denim jeans and matching flight jacket over a blinding white T-shirt, hair in a single braid down the back with red-and-yellow succulents at every turn, and lovely Flor, obviously the prize offering herself in this ceremony, flushed, in a knee-length, floral dress, around her neck a lei to match the gardenia in her hair. The two brides walked arm and arm with Charles who was to give them to each other.

Bringing up the rear was Cherry, representing the Feminist Wicca and acting that day as acolyte to Danny Mae.

The procession reached the floral arbor at the foot of the garden. The music stopped. In the hush, Sue thought she heard the distant rap of a Ferrari receding in the direction of the Richard M. Nixon Freeway. She heaved a sigh somewhere between sadness and relief.

Danny, being the only one with a theological mentality (as opposed to merely mystical, of which there were plenty), brought the intended couple together under a flowered arbor. After a brief ceremony of their own invention, Flor and Evelyn were pronounced married.

The rites completed, Flor and Evelyn kissed, maybe a little prolonged for any traditional ceremony, but not nearly long enough for that collection of guests. When the whistles stopped, Cherry intervened with glasses for the couple and filled them with red wine from her carafe. They drank, and smashed the glasses in the barbecue.

The recessional was led by three Hare Krishnas in white robes, swinging their smoking censors and chanting, "Hare Krishna, Hare Krishna, Krishna Krishna Hare, Hare."

That about satisfied everyone's expectations of ceremony.

At the top of the steps Flor and Evelyn stood arm in arm. Evelyn announced in her clear voice, "Let the party begin!"

After kissing the newlyweds, Sue drifted by the punch, Danny's contribution to the reception. "I had a cup of this myself about an hour ago, and I wonder…," said Danny as she handed Sue a half-filled paper cup, "…if you would connect with Allan's Market for another couple of gallons of orange juice. This stuff is a little heavy on the mescaline." That accounts for the variations in memory of this occasion. The ensuing celebration was sober by Venice standards. There was only one arrest—Santa Claus got high and lost on Main Beach. After he was bailed out and returned from Venice Division, the party lasted another full day.

Still wearing her striped jacket and white but wrinkled pants, Sue stood barefoot in the kitchen trying to summon up breakfast. What she got was her usual vision of Sapho.

It had been a lifetime, maybe even as much as six weeks, since the Big Movie crew had gathered to see their product in its final edited version. Sue had given up hope of ever again seeing Sapho. Indeed, she had nearly stopped pining. Unless one is a simpleton one does not long for any heterosexual or bisexual woman.

Nevertheless, there was Ground Zero Herself, quietly leaning against the door-jam, watching Sue wind a tea-bag around a spoon to squeeze out the last vital drop, and chuckling softly. "I didn't know you could cook," Sapho whispered.

Sue nearly jumped out of her skin. "Whoop! Don't sneak up on me like that! As for my cooking, it's a recipe from my grand-mother. Care for a cup?"

"Don't mind if I do," responded Sapho. After a brazen kiss and a gratis grind the two women settled on the floor in Sue's studio-bedroom. Sapho set her cup on the silver-caster, stirred in a couple of saccharin, and began what she had come for. "I saw you at Mick Jagger's party, and I saw you at Goldie Glitters' Thirtieth Birthday and at yesterday's wedding."

Sue smiled into Sapho's laughing eyes and continued the dia-logue. "It has been an interesting season already, hasn't it."

"You seem to get all the good invites."

"In my own way I guess I'm something of a social butterfly."

"Can you get me an invitation to Nickey the Easter Bunny's Resurrection Brunch?" There, Sapho had said it, and all she had to do was wait for the answer.

"The invites are all out. You should have seen Nickey in his giant rabbit suit, sitting on the passenger seat of his orange Honda motorcycle with Gary driving him all over town to hand-deliver the beautiful hand-written cards. I can bring a guest."

"If you could…. As a film-maker interested in the off-center, I have a professional imperative to get around more than most."

Before obsession took complete charge of Sue's life, she found herself with Sapho at Nickey's buffet, loading their plates with souffle and fruit salad.

"Isn't that a friend of yours?" Sapho asked with a glance into a far corner.

"My god! Yes!" It was Juice, with Patty, and so high she could neither speak nor care where she was. "Can you manage the egg hunt alone? I have to do something about this."

"Of course. Come over for egg salad sandwiches this evening. Isn't that Danny coming through the food line?"

Sue caught Danny at the fruit salad. "Yeah, I see it, too," said Danny. "Let's go over and eat with Sapho awhile. When they split out of here, I have an idea where they'll go. You and I will get Juice out of there and take her home."

"What's going on?" asked Sapho in a research mode.

"Well," answered Danny, "the big one is Kim's old lady from the Bay. She hates us because we take good care of Kim. The little one is Juice, Highland House pet, who it seems is a lot more needy and vulnerable than I suspected."

"I see," said Sapho. "I know a cat who drags half-consumed birds around the whole neighborhood."

"You got the idea. If we can't do anything else, we still have to mop up the carnage. You'll excuse us?" Danny wiped the fruit salad from the corners of her mouth, and she and Sue were gone.

Twenty minutes later they heaved in the door of an apartment on Pacific Coast Highway, just as Patty was loading to shoot up Juice again. "For Christ's sake," Danny shouted. "You animal! You want to kill her?"

"Oh, she's a lot tougher than she looks," said Patty. "Besides, she likes it."

"We don't like it!" Sue shouted. She and Danny led Juice out to the hearse, took her home and let her nod around the place until she would eat a couple of burgers. Then they let her sleep the rest of it off while all of Highland House basked in the usual disarray at Gay Beach.

92

Jan at the hamburger stand handed Sue her lunch with a grim piece of news. "When you get down to the water, tell them the black and whites are on the way!" Wasting no time, Sue kicked off her sandals and ran, as well as anyone can, across the hundred yards of deep sand toward Gay Beach, otherwise known as Nude Beach.

On the way she passed the men's latrine and a green hillock, upon which sat two male figures with slick hair, double-breasted black suits and pointy shoes. They were looking through binoculars at the semi-nude figures on Gay Beach, as if they had never before seen tits and cocks. At the same time a single file of four southward-bound black-and-white four-wheel-drive trucks did a right turn off Ocean Front Walk and proceeded four abreast across the sand to the sea.

"Suits on, everybody! The sand-fuzz are coming!" Sue hollered as soon as she got to the patchwork of blankets and towels with their loads of unemployed nudity.

Danny looked up in a state between ennui and contentment. "The good guys all know us, and the bad guys all leave us alone."

"If you don't put your top on, you'll go to jail. For heaven's sake get dressed!"

Hoping to allay Sue's fears, but not doing a very good job, Danny explained: "Que sera, sera, Sue. Jail is something we do every so often, and I guess it's time for their token sweep of the beach. It keeps the in-town squares happy, and gives the Public Defender practice at plea-bargaining."

The black-and-whites began at the pile of rocks in the surf at the border between Venice and Santa Monica, and ran south about fifty yards. There they stopped to handcuff Danny, Evelyn, Nola, and for good measure Charles, and took them away to the Venice Division police station.

When the public defender got there and saw all that skin she shook her head in desperation. "I'm really tired of trying this case over and over. With your permission I won't plea-bargain it this time. Maybe after a real court decision they'll leave you guys in peace."

"Don't ask me," said Juice in answer to Sue's questions. "All I know is we're having a meeting of the Maa-fia. It's about selling Highland House and going to jail. Can you and Karen get over here? Right now."

No one knew precisely what a lot in the Canals was worth, but $100,000 was a safe guess. If Danny was selling Highland House you could bet she was in big trouble.

They found Danny in the yard with the garden hose watering the neighborhood ducks who enjoyed a fresh-water bath every so often and needed something besides the brackish canal water to drink.

"What's this nonsense about selling the house? You can't mean it!" Karen said.

"It's not as bad as it sounds," Danny said. "Let's go inside and I'll tell you the whole story." She watered the crop of dolls' hands and sprinkled the row of feet by the doorstep before rolling up the hose for the day. Inside, she settled everyone in the living room and began the story. "Briefly, they finally caught up with me and I'm going to jail."

"Jail?" said Sue. "You go to jail monthly. But selling the house? They must be the Internal Revenue Service, at least."

"It wasn't the Feds, it was the State of California. They busted me for welfare fraud."

"Whew! I'm glad it wasn't for dealing dope. But welfare fraud?"

"How do you think I keep this houseful of people eating and off the street? It was a stupid mistake. I had a mythical company with a mythical employee who was collecting a not-so-mythical Disability award. When he 'got well' and 'quit', I submitted all that paper work and thought it was finished, except I neglected to dissolve the company. Eventually they noticed, looked into the situation and uncovered the whole scam. Naturally, I didn't want them nosing any more into my affairs, so I plea-bargained down from a felony to a misdemeanor by offering to pay back all the money. Sentence was reduced to six months, beginning in a couple of weeks."

Sue was still worried. "What a shame you have to sell the house. What's going to happen to everyone with Highland House gone? Isn't there some other way we can raise the money?"

"Actually, the money is coming from my cousin. But he doesn't want visibility either, so I'm pretending to sell the house so the court doesn't ask any questions. While I'm in jail, I can use your help."

"Anything...within reason."

"If I give you the checks, can you mail the house payments on time?"

"Easy," said Sue. "And we can also drop by on visitor's days. I don't think I could survive going to jail. You must be terrified!"

"Terrified. Yes," Danny admitted.

In another few days Danny reported to Sybil Brand Institute For Women, and they locked her up.

On a sunny Sunday three months later, long before Danny was expected out, Sue rolled out at dawn (not more than three hours after she and Karen had stumbled in from a deafening hard-rock Saturday night in town) to polish her stock of jewelry for a lucrative day at the beach. Ocean Front Walk would be jammed with Angelenos and tourists looking good and ready to join the fashion parade. It was the first Sunday of the month. The net spendable in some pockets would buy something of intrinsic value rather than the usual T-shirts. With any luck, Sue could come home with the month's rent and a week's expenses.

She put two trays of rings and a display board of pendants in a brown paper bag and headed for the beach. By eleven o'clock she had put away breakfast at the Germans' and was dozing on the grass in front of the Sidewalk Cafe listening to a woman playing her clarinet and watching a man juggling bowling balls. It would soon be time to go down to Terry's doorway to set up a tray or two. As she sat thinking, a black and white Harley Davidson rolled around the corner with a policeman in black breeches, polished black boots and leather gloves.

"You there! It's illegal to vend from city property!" he shouted from behind steel-rimmed sun glasses.

"I know that, sir. I wouldn't think of doing that," said Sue.

"Just shut up and stay where you are. You're under arrest. Hand over your identification." He garbled something into his radio and the station squawked back. "Aha! You have eighteen warrants against you. A patrol car is on the way to pick you up."

My god, *she* was going off to jail! She couldn't believe it, and neither could the crowd collecting to watch this strange affair. She got the attention of a complete stranger in the front row. "Please call my roommate, and ask her to come and bail me out. I haven't more than five dollars on me."

The woman was writing down Karen's phone number and promising someone would rescue Sue when the black and white wheeled around the corner and parked with all four wheels on the grass she was accused of violating. Obviously justice was not only blind but schizophrenic.

One officer put her paper bag in the trunk while the other one cuffed her hands behind her and pushed her into the back seat beside the third partner. Off they went to Venice Division police station where she was patted down, photographed, finger-printed and booked. "So," said the booking officer, "you're a real scoff-law, aren't you?"

"I'm not a scoff-law!" Sue said. "And anyway you haven't any right to call me nasty names."

"Whatever. We haven't any room for you here so you're going to Van Nuys."

Van Nuys? How would Karen ever find her there? What if the lady hadn't called Karen after all? These and other vital questions clogged her mind as she rolled around in the back seat, unable to keep proper balance with her hands cuffed behind her. The cuffs were too tight. Sue was scared and miserable.

At Van Nuys she got the attention of the admitting officer.

"Listen," said Sue. "I have a neurological disorder called narcolepsy. This means I have seizures every four to six hours." At the word 'seizures' the officer stopped what he was writing, turned white and stared at her. Sue knew she had hit on a good way to exercise some small control of her fate behind bars. She resumed her monologue. "I think it would be a good idea to put me in a cell with a padded cot for me to lie down. Otherwise I'm going to fall over and hit my head on something."

"You're right. First I'll have to get your condition certified by someone. I'll send you over to the sheriff's nurse."

Delicious. She was making herself into a problem. The nurse was off duty over the weekend, so they headed for the emergency hospital. After waiting half an hour for a case of heat exhaustion to be treated, she finally got her retinas looked at and her papers signed.

On the way back to the Van Nuys station, the third partner, the one in the back seat, got talkative. "You know, this is a real opportunity for me, working in Venice for the afternoon, getting to see what it's like down there. How come you chose to lead the life you lead?"

Sue felt like something between a bug behind glass and a convicted assassin. "Choose this life? Are you kidding? Nobody chooses poverty! Jobs just disappear, and you find yourself on the street. I never thought I'd ever be poor, but here I am. Luckily, I can earn a bare living making jewelry until the computer programming jobs open up again. When that happens, I'll be able to buy and sell you and your dumb cop job. Pray you never lose your job."

The cop in the passenger's seat up front who had been listening with one ear, turned slightly and gave her a look of approval.

Back at Van Nuys, she found herself alone in a new tank with about six cots. The ticking on the fully stuffed mattresses was clean, and she sat down on the one nearest the pay phone. They had taken away all of her belongings except the change in her pocket. One by one she dialed her friends, but no one was home. Mercifully, the Establishment gave her dime back if she hung up with no answer. Everyone was still at the beach.

For as long as possible, she put off using the toilet. It was clean all right, but there was no paper and it was right out in the open. Finally, urgency overcame modesty. The relief relaxed her somewhat, and she indulged in the luxury of rinsing her face and hands in the stream from the drinking fountain.

For a while she sat on the edge of the cot wishing they hadn't taken away her comb. Did they think she could escape or commit suicide with it? Prisoner With Teeth Marks Found Dead In Solitary. How's that for a headline?

She dialed home again, and was listening to the ring-tones when the guard shook the bars. "Come on, then. You're going home." They gave back everything, including the paper bag with all of its jewelry. She signed the day-book beside her name, and she was let loose in the lobby, just like that.

From across the room came a shrill, "Sue!"

"Karen! Thank god for your smiling little face!" They hugged so hard it would have been embarrassing anyplace else. "How in hell did you find me?"

"The lady from the beach called until she connected. Can you believe that? I got her name and phone for you. I phoned around until I found you. You can't imagine how hard it is to wrestle up one hundred and sixty dollars cash for bail on a late Sunday afternoon!"

"Oh, god! I'm crashing!" was all Sue could say. Karen led her to William Randolph and got her in through the corpse door just in time to crash out on the back deck. Karen put the new Carole King tape on the machine, and drove slowly home.

Arraignment was in East L.A. the next morning. Karen dropped Sue at the steps to the court, and saying something about parking and an errand, disappeared around the corner.

Before Sue knew it, she was standing in front of the judge, last in a line of seven people, all accused of the same crime. There was some legal mumbo-jumbo, and then she heard the judge saying. "I have here eighteen warrants for parking violations against your International Travelall. How do you plead?"

"There's been some mistake, Your Honor. I don't own a Travelall. I drive a '58 Cadillac."

"This vehicle seems to be registered to a Rodriguez. Your

name is Rodriguez?"

"No, your honor. It's Richards."

"Hmm. Yes. I see what you mean. All right, case dismissed. Pick up your money from the bailiff. Next?"

She finished up with the bailiff, and turned to walk toward the main exit from the court. There, big as life, were Karen and Danny, laughing and smiling like a couple of cheap comedians.

They all hugged, and Sue said, "Danny! What are you doing out so early?"

"You have a few things to answer for yourself!" she said as they walked toward William Randolph. Danny's mind was elsewhere. "Is it OK if we stop off in East L.A. for Silver?"

"Well, sure." Sue started the lovely and familiar engine.

"Who the heck is Silver?"

"Just wait and see! I'll tell the whole story to everyone at once when we're home."

No more than an hour later they were back in Danny's garden again. Somebody filled a wash tub with ice and cans of beer, someone else filled the plastic wading pool with water, and everyone stripped down to nothing. With no ado nor specific invitation, Silver slipped out of the kitchen naked, with a plate stacked with burritos. In every way Silver was Danny's opposite. Days in the sun had turned her brown skin dark to match her hair. Where noisy Danny was a city girl, Silver was more comfortable in the peaceful desert. After passing around the burritos with smiles, Silver stepped into the cool water and assumed a sitting position between Danny's legs, a place from which she was to rule Danny and Highland House for some time to come. Everyone settled in for a wet and wonderful afternoon welcoming the jailbirds home.

First they heard the details of Danny's incarceration: "So here's how I met Silver. The first thing I remember was standing in the lunch line. There she was, this Aztec Apache princess Silver person, looking at me like I was charmed. I could hardly eat, thinking about her, and then someone handed me a note from her. It was full of mushy stuff, and she said to volunteer for the infirmary. She said it was disgusting duty, but that would give us a chance to work out ways to be alone together.

"Finally they locked me in my cell with my room mate. As I stood looking at her and the guards, it hit me: The guards were worse off than I was. Those poor suckers were stuck in this stinking joint for life! I was going to get out in a few months. In the meantime, my life would be a lot easier if I made it my business to make their lives as pleasant as possible.

"I looked around for the most disgusting jobs, and remembered what Silver had written. So I volunteered for the infirmary. There they like help who can read and write. As soon as I got to the wards, Silver was there in person, with supper trays for the patients. I was really flustered, you can imagine, but Silver was cool. She knew the head nurse was lesbian. From then on we had time alone in our own space pretty often.

"Anyhow, for any unspeakable job, I made sure they called for Danny. I willingly cleaned up some of the vilest messes you have ever seen. I can't even describe all the disgusting mixtures of body fluids. I risked physical damage to feed and comfort women who were so emaciated and crazy they should have been buried or in the loony bin, but were actually chained to the wall instead.   :

"One morning a police car rolled in and let out the ugliest, most dangerous-looking woman I have ever seen. None of the guards wanted to risk going anywhere near her, so naturally they called for me. I took her by the hand, and she calmed a little. Then I put both arms around her. God, she smelled awful! She didn't seem to know English, so I tried Spanish, telling her I wouldn't let anyone hurt her, that she would get lunch, clean clothes and a nice bath. But she let me lead her to one of the guards and put their hands together. I was a hero.

"I worked overtime making Sybil Brand Institute a better place to be. All my time was 'good time', so they had to send me home in three months."

After several minutes Sue broke the silence. "I don't know how you did it. I think I would go out of my mind, in prison all that time."

Danny popped the top off another beer and settled back in the inner tube with the sprinkler in her lap. "I owe it all to Silver. She taught me to keep my fat mouth shut. Surviving jail is a matter of protecting your own mind. You have to do that in your own way. It seems to me you were doing OK for only one day in custody. I loved the way you dragged that whole carload of cops all over the county. Inside of another week, you would probably have made yourself into a jail-house lawyer."

Danny in charge

Chapter 13

It was still too early on a weekend day for all but the beach regulars. As Sue and Toots rounded the corner onto Ocean Front Walk they heard first the clang of symbols and the chant of the Hare Krishnas as they marched along the tide line. Counterpoint to that was the puff-and-slap of paddle tennis on the courts, punctuated by the percussion of bar-bells falling against concrete at Muscle Beach. On the sand, two skin divers did their Tai Chi Chuan to the morning rhythms.

Around the corner at the liquor store the clerk counted out a pile of change being offered for an early, desperate bottle. When it was her turn, Sue bought her morning's nicotine fix and scored a cigar box for her treasury. On her way back home, she stopped in her tracks. Something was definitely wrong with *Venice In The Snow*.

Venice in the Snow is a huge mural painted by The Fine Arts Squad on a sturdy apartment house across from Muscle Beach on Ocean Front Walk. The picture is a life-size, realistic landscape showing Ocean Front Walk and its buildings, adjoining sand and notable citizens shivering in six inches of snow. The painting merges into the beach sand so realistically that you start looking for yourself in the picture. Some people are so disoriented that they walk into the wall.

Something new had been added to *Venice in the Snow*. There in the foreground was a mechanism which could be a snow plow! As she walked toward the wall she got dizzy. Her mind thought she was still walking into the picture and was confused when the perspective seemed to change. The snow plow changed size and viewpoint. It was real! And in fact it was a bulldozer sitting in a hole right in front of the wall. Someone was going to erect a new building which would hide*Venice in the Snow* forever! What a revolting idea!

Surrounding this vulgarity was a chain-link fence and inside that was a heavy red Doberman, with crisp docked ears, devotedly guarding with a lonely, lean and thirsty look. Toots and the Dobie were playing nosey and wagging.

"What do you say Toots? Shall we get this pooch a nice drink of water? She looks so miserable." By the time Sue and Toots found a bottle in the trash can and got back to the Dobie, someone else had been there with a shovel and had stolen both the dog and its water dish.

Danny's nudity was cooling off in a wash-tub full of water while a large, red Doberman happily ran through the sprinkler. "Meet Ruby." Ruby romped over to Juice for a scratching. "It's a wise dog who knows who she belongs to."

Sue squatted to have a look at Ruby. "She's a handsome beast."

"And so good and sweet," Juice said. "I think she was a kid's dog before some jerk put her out to work in that crummy pit."

"Well, any kid lucky enough to have a good-looking Doberman like Ruby had better keep her on a nice, leather leash." She pressed a wad of bills into Juice's hand. "So what else have you been up to?"

"Paddle tennis hustling," said Juice while maintaining a thank you in her soft, brown eyes.

"Paddle tennis hustling?"

"There's always a sucker who doesn't know I was on the tennis team at home last year."

"In that case," whispered Sue, "you had better throw away those old tennies before you trip on the fringe. A pair of new Adidas will clean up your act." She folded up two twenties, slipped them into Juice's shirt pocket and got back a young woman's kiss to warm her tired old heart.

"It's from Mother," Danny said, reading a letter. "Wants me to visit her in Florida."

"Florida! You just get home from the slammer, and you're leaving?" It was hard to tell whether Juice was madder than she was sad, but she certainly was disappointed. "You wouldn't do that, would you, Danny?"

"Don't get over-wrought, kid. Being as you're the nearest she'll have to a granddaughter, Mother has forked over. There's a ticket here for you, too."

"You mean it? I'm going, too? I've never been to Florida. I've never been anywhere at all. Oh, well. I can't go, and that's that." Juice slumped onto the grass, broken-hearted, with an arm around the dog Ruby who nuzzled into her armpit.

"I've been gone quite a while, but...I guess it doesn't take any more than overnight to get a big thing going, does it."

"No, no. It isn't that, although it might have been, a time or two. Just so you don't start taking me for granted. I can't go to Florida without Ruby, so there!"

Sue saw Juice in a new light, as the really young person she truly was. "I had no idea you were so attached to Ruby."

"Who do you think dug her out of *Venice in the Snow*, with her tennis paddle? Who feeds her, washes and brushes and trims her fur and loves her?"

After listening to that part of it all, Danny turned to Juice. "Where I go, you go. Where you go, Ruby goes. We're a circus act, Danny and the Kidnapped. We'll rent a travel cage, and Ruby can ride in the baggage compartment. How's that?"

"Make Ruby ride in that cold, dark, noisy old baggage compartment? Nothing doing. She'd never speak to me again. Can't she ride with us passengers, if we buy her a seat?"

"They don't allow that, honey." Sue explained. "The only dogs allowed in the passenger section are guide dogs."

A hush spread over the back yard. "You mean, like a Seeing Eye dog," Danny whispered.

"Shazam! That's it! How do we do that, Danny?" asked Juice.

"How do we do that, Sue?" asked Danny.

"How do you do what?" queried the truly puzzled Sue.

"How do I pretend to be blind, dummy!" Leave it to Juice to be crystal clear.

"That's a pretty good idea, Juice. I used to have a blind friend with a dog. I could tell you about him, and you could take it from there."

"The floor, or grass, is yours, Sue." Danny said, and Sue began. "You can have Ruby on her regular leash. Without the heavy steel harness, a guide dog isn't working. She's a regular old loveable pooch. Ruby can be a very protective guide dog on vacation from its usual trade of guiding, which will make sense since Danny can lead you around by the arm. You guys can practice that, so that Juice can get to trust your lead. Ruby does all the verbal commands, and she's very cool around strangers so she's a natural.

"Better cover your eyes completely with really dark glasses. You can't afford to let anyone see your normal-looking eyes. If the glasses are so dark you stumble, so much the better."

"If anyone asks, tell them you have been blind for five years. That should explain your lavish body language, and anything you might let slip about sports."

"Have you a virgin pair of jeans and new-ish tennies? Blind girls don't rough-house around much. Scrub your hands and manicure your nails, and don't let anyone see the calluses!

"Eating. You are allowed to push your food onto your fork, and look around with your hands. Practice this. Do as much as possible with eyes closed."

The magnitude of the undertaking stunned everyone into prolonged silence. Finally Juice nodded firmly and affirmatively. "It'll work. Yes, it'll work, Danny, if you leave it all up to me, if you'll do exactly what I tell you."

"How's this for a bossy kid! You don't trust me? Who's the grown-up here, anyway?"

"Don't anyone answer that," Sue interjected. "As a matter of fact, I agree with Juice. She's the blind one, who would be the expert anyway. Danny you can be her aunt, a doting, over-wrought aunt."

"I know when I'm outnumbered, but I reserve the right to veto at any point I deem it necessary."

As the day of departure approached, Juice called to confirm their ride to the airport in the hearse. "So how is Danny holding up? Is she giving you any trouble?" Sue asked.

"Danny's doing as well as can be expected...."

At that point Danny grabbed the phone. "You wouldn't believe this kid. She's been spending every morning at the library, reading up on how they train guide dogs, and how it is to be blind. I think I'm in good hands."

On get-away-day, Sue let them off at the curb in front of Delta Airlines, and watched them move slowly and firmly into the crowded ticket area. Two beautiful women with an equally attractive red Doberman had to attract attention. After she had circled the airport six times, the flight time passed, and they did not re-appear at the curb, she assumed everything was under control.

The following month, Sue was waiting for them by the curb at LAX. The two women had all new clothes, and Ruby had a new leash and a bandanna around her neck, but aside from that they were the same old friends.

Danny let Ruby in the 'live' door, and she and Juice settled into the front seat. "So how did it go?" Sue inquired anxiously.

"Perfect! This kid had all the answers for everyone, and kept the whole plane amused with blind stories."

"The only trouble was with Danny. She wouldn't read me the book I wanted to hear." Juice was grumbling, but had the vestige of a smile.

"Rita Mae Brown? Aloud on Delta Airlines? You think I'm some kind of crazy?"

Chapter 14

The rumble of Nola's Honda chopper stopped at the entrance to the driveway and dissolved into a crunch of tires on sand. Beer cans clinking against each other and boots on the steps announced Nola arriving for her usual late morning stop at Karen and Sue's place.

Sue looked up from her work and screamed, "My god, Nola! What in hell happened to you!"

One eye was swollen almost shut, there were bandages across her nose and over her eyebrow, she was black and blue in various places, and worst of all, she was smiling on one side only. "Gotta get offa that bike!" Nola muttered. The open eye was twinkling all right, so anyone could see she meant it.

"Tell me you didn't pile up."

"I didn't pile up. You know I ride better than that. Last night me and Dean got into it with about five Hell's Angels, at the bar next to the Germans'. I admit it, we had too much beer and got pretty smart-ass, but one of them couldn't take a joke, and started kicking my bike around. So I started kicking his ankles around, and then we were into it."

"Wouldn't you like something cold for that eye? It doesn't look like you're going to work until Monday, does it."

"A plastic bag full of ice would be nice. And you're right, its sick-leave time."

While Sue popped a tray of cubes for the eye and a bottle of aspirin for general purposes, Nola dialed her night time job at the Bacchanal and muttered something about beer and black eyes. Then she sat quietly nursing her wounds and in a few moments continued her story. "So naturally I stopped at the bar

107

for breakfast this morning. One of the Hell's Angels was back, too. He was laughing and laughing. A good thing for him I felt too bad to lay one on him. Finally he said I looked pretty bad, but the other guys were looking in the mirror at something even worse! *And* he said that none of the Hell's Angels in the State of California would ever bother Dean and me again."

When they finished laughing Sue asked, "So why are you talking about giving up biking, now that you are socially acceptable, so to speak?"

"I don't want to give up my bike, just add in a surfer's van. With my two jobs, I'm always looking for a place to change clothes, and my clothes are always all messy when I take them out of the side-bags and put them on."

"Now, if you had a rolling dressing room...."

"You got it! And after I've been drinking, I need a place to sleep some of it off before driving home to Sapho's or to Thea's."

"It's the perfect solution. You know how I worry about you and that bike and the booze."

"And there are lots of times I go to Thea's place when I don't feel like it at all, just so I can safely sober up and don't end up in the gutter some place. Let's have a look at my bank balance."

Sue walked to the closet, reached into the hole where Nola kept the shoe box with her bank book and tips. Nola opened it and found her check book all alone on the bottom. "Amazing! That brand new Ford Econoline van won't take half of what's here. Can you still ride a bike?"

"Can I still fuck?" said Sue.

"Then let's go to the Santa Monica Ford agency and write them a check for that green van I've been looking at. You can ride the bike back to it's garage at Sapho's, and I'll bring you home from there."

It was nearly noon by the time they got back to Rialto Street. Nola's face was too cut and too puffy and her brain too sore for her noon-time beer; but she came in anyway and let Sue pack a fresh bag of ice for the swollen parts and swab away the fresh blood. "I know the green van will be good for you, but you've got to promise you'll never drive when you're drunk. The few times

I've let you drive the hearse under the influence, I worried more than I ever let on."

"I think I maintain pretty well."

"Well, you don't."

"OK, no drunk driving. Now there's another favor you can do me," she said. "Can you go to the doctor with me in a couple of hours?"

"Sure, if you think you need me. I think it's smart to have someone look at your face," Sue said.

"There's more to it than that. Since I'm a new patient she wants to do a complete physical. If you're not there I'll faint when I watch her draw blood and all that."

Sue laughed in spite of herself. "Anyone tough enough to stand up to the Hell's Angels probably doesn't need me to hold her hand, but what do I know?"

Sue waited in the anteroom, promising to come running if Nola called. Eventually she emerged with a new and smaller strip covering three stitches near her eyebrow, and smears of medication on the scrapes. Her smile was still one-sided, but both eyes were sparkling.

"So, how did she say you are?" Sue inquired.

"The blood and piss departments are OK, but the pap smear will take a week to find out."

"She did a pelvic? One of the secondary benefits of illness?"

Nola shifted around in her chair, unable to distinguish self-consciousness from pleasure. "No one ever explains things to me before-hand. But I've got something called clamydia growing you-know-where, so I'll have to go to the drug store. I think I would have freaked out if it hadn't been a woman doctor. She says I have to quit smoking or cut down a lot. I have to start using a filter, a Tar Guard, which is like cutting down to a half."

"Maybe I should do the same thing," mused Sue.

"Would you? It would make it a whole lot easier. Maybe we could get Karen, too." She carefully touched some of the tender spots and inspected the corneas of her eyes. "Next time I go drinking I'll wear my catcher's mask."

Chapter 15

The name of the game was Slow Pitch Softball. The Venice team's uniform was red numbers on black shirts and shorts, black shoes and pink Ace elastic bandages, all supplied by their sponsor the Bacchanal Bar in Hollywood, and the Venice Free Family Clinic. Nola, the catcher, was bandaged around her right thigh to hold in place the tendon she had stretched during the summer she was runner-up world champion surfer-girl. Evelyn, in right field, always wore an Ace on her ankle, to help avoid the inevitable sprain. Danny, in left field, had been free from damage for two seasons, until the week Charles registered people to vote with the Peace and Freedom Party. If you registered, you got a free Quaalude from the half-gallon box-full which his shrink had donated to the cause. Danny registered, and wrecked her knee playing football in the surf.

Karen was whole and healthy at first base. Manager and coach of this rag-tag mob were Jan and her lover Dee respectively (also owners of Jan and Dee's Hamburgers at the beach). Unfortunately, Dee was self-destructive, a personality defect incompatible with coaching. Every time they got a run in, Dee would change the line-up. This is poor tactics and poorer psychology if you expect to win. In spite of their coach, the team always played hard and with good spirit.

The Venice team had a large and loyal following, or possibly that bunch of bar-flies hung around the team because of the after-game parties at the winning sponsor's bar. Since the Venice gang didn't win often, they and their fans were well-acquainted in the bars all over the county. Leave it to them to turn losing into winning.

Sue enjoyed the benefits of being a loyal fan but, actually, she hated softball. Still, she went along whenever Nola needed someone to deflect the groupies which she tended to collect.

Sue stopped at Highland house for the team. The afternoon was beginning with an argument. Danny was doing her best to lay down the law. "No, Juice, you can't come along. If the cops decide to raid the bar, off you'll go to the Juvenile Authority, and I'll be doing five to ten for contributing to the delinquency of a minor."

"But I don't have to go to the bar after the game," countered Juice, who knew how to argue with Danny. "I can stay in the hearse and wait."

"Well, OK," said Danny. "Bring along your book," (Juice was among the few who read much of anything), "and bring Ruby. It's a tough neighborhood over there." (It was tough everywhere.) Once they got going, Danny relented as often as not.

Meanwhile Nola and her green van picked up the rest of the team including Taco and Nicole, both of whom lived in other parts of Venice. No sooner had Nola gotten under way than Taco started in: "Can't we please stop at a Seven Eleven? I'm having a Slurpy attack."

"N-O!" Nola barked. "Last time we stopped you stole a candy bar, and it took me half an hour to talk the manager out of calling the police."

"Can I help it," Taco bragged, "if I come from a long line of brazen thieves?" Both of her parents were in the joint in Arizona, and she was living with an aunt on parole from Sybil Brand. Taco couldn't spell right, not even in Spanish, but she was a champion base stealer and third-base coach.

The last team member, Nicole, lived in a black feminist commune. She was so good at auto mechanics she should have been a chicana. She was overweight by at least 100 pounds and couldn't play softball worth a damn. But being on the team was very important to Nicole. She played with such heart and so enthusiastically that she was a real boost to morale. None of the Venice girls would ever play at all for Dee if Nicole weren't on the team.

111

When they were all parked near the park, Sue took her time locking up the hearse and walking over to the van where Nola was still lacing up her cleats and wrapping her thigh. While she wrapped she discussed with Nicole, who was worried. "If Dee won't let me play, let me just dress out and sit on the bench, or even just sit there in my regular clothes. You're team captain, Nola. Can't you fix it for me?"

"You know how we count on you for morale, and for that you are a whole lot better on the field than sitting on that silly bench. I'll see what Dee says. If she says OK, you can get my keys from Sue and dress out here in my van."

Nicole's round face brightened and she ran happily toward the ball field while Sue and Nola strolled along more slowly. "Is Dee going to go for this?" Sue wondered.

"Maybe. We'll need Nicole's spirit today."

"This Valley team is plenty tough," Sue agreed.

"This will be the world's shortest and dullest game. The league rule is that if one team is twelve points ahead at the end of any inning, the game is forfeited. This thing could last as long as two innings"

"So," moaned Sue, "I won't have time for burritos."

"Maybe Taco and Nicole will make the trip out here worth while. Anyhow, you can amuse yourself watching the Valley pitcher. I've had the hots for her for two years now, but I can never get anywhere."

From the stands Sue watched Danny hitting practice flies to the team, and tried unsuccessfully to lip-read Nola's conference with Dee. Then suddenly Nola's face broke into a smile and she hollered "Nicole, dress out!" No one had any trouble hearing Nicole's shrieks of delight. In no time she was back, in uniform, and the fans were cheering as she assumed her place on the bench with the starting line-up.

It was the bottom of the first, Valley fourteen, Venice Zip, one out. It was Taco's turn at bat, and the fans roared "Taco, Taco," demanding the kind of action they knew she was capable of. As she picked up the bat Taco determined to take the first pitch, no matter how good or bad it was. Maybe a little barrio bravado would create enough confusion to get her to first.

112

She cinched up on the bat. As champion base-stealer she thrived on the kind of tense situation she was about to create. The pitch. Bam! Not a bad hit, a fast low ball that skipped into center field where it created the desired confusion. Taco hot-footed toward first,

"Slide, Taco! Slide!" came the advice from the stands. Taco slid to first, safe.

Now the fans went nuts. "Nicole, Nicole." She was actually going to play ball, and she was so happy she could hardly stand it.

Before the pitch Nola moved in as first base coach, prepared to talk Nicole all the way home if necessary. The fans and the team were out of their minds. As Nicole stepped up to the plate, Nola exercised her coaching and captain's privilege and strode over to the pitcher's mound. Nola and the pitcher stood there a few minutes forehead to forehead. Sue tried to lip-read what they were saying, but only got a string of ah's, ee's and oo's.

The Pitch. In the zone, strike.

Another pitch, slower. Strike.

More pitches. Balls, Nicole walked! Taco moved on to second, mumbling something about being deprived of some action.

Danny stepped to the plate. She took the first pitch and bunted. They still argue the wisdom of that move, with her bum knee, ace bandage and all, but the move flustered the shortstop who threw to first. Danny slid to first base and let out such a cry you would think she had broken her neck. Nicole advanced to second, Taco to third.

Danny was out but the first basewoman was so flustered by all that noise from Danny that she forgot the wisdom of getting the ball off to the pitcher. In all the confusion Taco was tip-toeing home! Only then did the first basewoman peg the ball toward the plate.

"Slide, Taco slide!" She slid feet first and was safe at home— except that her foot was bent up under her. Such a scream you could hear all the way to Burbank! Nola and the pitcher rushed to Taco's side, examined her and shook their heads. Taco had a busted leg, and they carried her back to the bench. In all the flurry, Nicole made it to third, in position to score.

113

Little Karen trotted up to the plate, picked up the bat, and pulled up her stockings. She never did find a pair small enough. Now, the strike zone for Karen was relatively small and close to the ground. Also, Karen was a lefty. When the pitch came it was slow and easy, duck soup for Karen's hard bat.

Away the ball went to the Left Field, who was sleeping as in any other game. When she finally got control of herself, she pegged the ball to first. It should have been to home, because Nicole was on her way there!

Bedlam! "Slide, Nicole!" thundered the fans in the stands. "Slide, slide!" hollered Nola, now coaching from homeplate. And Nicole not only slid, she slid head first, two hundred and thirty-five pounds of enthusiasm scattering a furrow of dust on everyone in the vicinity.

Karen was out at third, the game was over. The fans carried Nicole, sweaty and dusty, all the way to Nola's van where she rode in the co-pilot's seat all the way to the bar sponsoring the winning team.

Most of the team had settled into booths but had not ordered beer when at last Nola came in the back door alone. She climbed up onto the bar and stood with her hands on her hips. She whistled for attention, then announced, "The crummy management of this crummy bar won't let Nicole come in on account of her skin color. I think that about finishes the afternoon, right?"

"Right" came the chorus, and the Venice team marched out en masse.

Being it was Sunday, the Hollywood Free Clinic was almost empty except for the doctor. While he heard the play-by-play, he set Taco's leg and cleaned up the scrapes on Nicole's arms. They finished the afternoon at their own sponsor's bar, the Bacchanal, in Hollywood.

As usual, Nola officiated at the back bar with Sue riding shot-gun by the service bar. As Nola leaned over to refresh her o.j. Sue whispered, "I'd give anything to know what in hell you said to that pitcher, just before she pitched to Nicole."

"I promised to sleep with her if she let Nicole run in."

114

Nola poured herself a cup of coffee and settled in the living room while Karen dressed out for paddle tennis. "Here," she said soberly to Sue, handing her a weathered tennis paddle. "You and I are playing doubles with Karen and Juice this morning." "Are you crazy? Or maybe you haven't seen me play." "You play well enough for my present purposes," Nola said, comfortingly. "They say Juice plays pretty well. I'd like to play her, but Karen has a shit fit every time I step out in the court with anyone else."

"You are aware, I'm sure, that Little Karen is in love with you?" Sue hated to open the subject, but there it was.

Nola shook her street-wise head very slowly. "No, Karen is in love with Sylvia. She's not in love with me, she's jealous of me as a tennis partner. And she's jealous of you and me because we're pals. Talk about a pain in the neck! What's more important in the local scheme of things, is Juice going to be around here a while longer or not?"

Sue squirmed around before answering. "I think of Juice as a permanent Venice institution."

"That's a relief," said Nola, bringing the conversation back to the matter of prime importance. "I might like to ask Juice to be my doubles partner in the tournament this summer, but I have to play against her before I can really judge her. I really need your help on this paddle tennis thing, so it has to be you and me against them this morning."

Before Sue could reply, Karen came out of her room. "Don't you think Sue needs to run around the court a little?" Nola asked. "We've got Juice for a fourth."

"Far fuckin' out!" said Karen, and they were on their way.

When they got to the courts, Juice was exercising inside the fence like a race-horse in a corral. There was a brief squabble over who was to be Nola's partner, but Nola settled it herself. "Come on, Sue. You and I can beat the socks off these two."

Juice assumed a "ready" stance behind the baseline. As the time for the serve approached, she jogged from one foot to the other with the footwork of a boxer, and never stopped until the point was won. As fast as paddle tennis is, she preferentially moved into the net, preparing for every receipt, returning the ball to her opponents vulnerable spot. Meanwhile, Karen played her usual game of 'bouncy ball.'

After they had played a few points, Nola flagged everyone to the bench. Seated between the two she announced, "Juice, you're dynamite. Karen, you have to hear this. I want Juice to be my doubles partner in the tournament this summer. What do you say, Juice?"

"Shazam! You bet!" Then Juice had the flash of an idea. "I'll do it, if you can get Dee to try me out for shortstop. If I make the team, Danny will have to let me go to the bars every game." She bounced the tennis ball up and down on her paddle, smugly waiting for Nola's answer.

"Hmm. In your uniform, you'll look like the rest of us. No one will think to question your age. Smart-ass kid, you got yourself a deal!"

After Juice had left, Karen spoke up. "I thought you and I did OK in the tournament last year."

Nola had a pained expression. "We practiced and practiced, but still didn't make it to the semi-finals. I think it's time a dyke team won the big prize for a change, and I think Juice and I are winners."

"It would have been fairer if you had told me I was competing with Juice just now," Karen complained.

"Juice didn't know, either. I had to see you two side-by-side to make up my mind," Nola said. But Karen was headed home in a huff.

When Sue and lunch-time arrived, Karen was still in her room sulking, with the open door inviting comforting, whether she deserved it or not. It was parsnips or nothing.

For a meat-and potatoes carnivore, Sue knew more about vegetables than she cared to admit. For a fledgling vegetarian, Karen was more devoted than knowledgeable. Her typical trip to the grocery store netted at least one weird veggie which she had no idea how to prepare or serve. It remained for Sue to show how it was done and generally assume future responsibility for cooking it.

Buttered parsnips are the perfect embodiment of Zen vegetable containing both the yin and the yang multiplexed. They are as delicious as they are cheap, and they are as cheap as they are bad-smelling in the pan.

The smell got Karen's attention when nothing else would. "Lunch?" she said, emerging from her self-imposed exile.

"Lunch," Sue confirmed as she messed around with smelly veggies in the hot pan. "I thought you deserved something you like." She spooned out two plate-loads of toasty brown parsnips. When Karen finally smiled, Sue put the question. "Well, have you decided to patch it up with Nola, or are you two going to be avoiding each other?"

Karen savored a few spoonfuls before answering. "If we don't forgive each other, who in hell else will?"

By that time the apartment smelled like a flat rock in a barn yard. Sue tried opening what she had always assumed was the front door and found it locked. Instead she threw open the front window and the back door as usual, letting the ocean breeze make the place sweet again.

"What's behind that mysterious locked door?" Sue wondered out loud.

"A stairway," Karen explained between slurps. "Before this house was converted to upper and lower apartments, the inside stairs made sense. Now we keep both doors locked, top and bottom, and use the outside stairs."

"Hmm. If you put up a rod inside there, you'd have a closet," Sue observed. "It seems like you could use some closet space around here."

"Or," said Karen slowly, "if I put in floor boards, I'd have a little office. A place to work on people's astrologies instead of messing up the living room..."

"...a place to lock up your dope stash," Sue suggested.

"...and a wall to pin up my maps, for when I'm working for the elves!" said Karen.

At that, Sue looked Karen square in the eye. "You did say 'elves.' Have you gone goofy?"

Karen was laughing so hard she could barely talk. "I knew you'd have trouble with that one. There's this commune in north Marin County. They're all women, and they claim they are real elves, the Irish kind. Each was born into a regular family of course, but eventually the rest of the elves found them and took them up one by one."

"Very strange," said Sue. "The mythological elves were suspected kidnappers, and were all very small. Do you suppose you are onto something here?"

"They are sure I'm an elf, too, and asked me to join. I wasn't anxious to join the troop, and begged off with some vague allusion to a conflict of interest with my Brownie Scout oath. Anyway they let me do work for them in their several old and established family businesses. At this stage in my life, work is work. Their money is at least as good as anyone else's. They do a little light manufacturing..."

"...which we might have guessed," said Sue.

"...but mostly they gather gold dust."

"Why doesn't that surprise me?"

"I do some of the gold business for them. They have deals with dentists all over the west coast, to get the old silver and gold fillings. I trip around for them about once a year. Which reminds me, I've got to get wheels pretty soon."

Sue laughed uproariously. "You mean, they didn't issue you a set of wings?"

"That's fairies, silly, and that's a whole other story! Let's go up to the roof for a few rays," Karen suggested. "If we take a nap, we might be ready for the gang in a while." Sue and Karen and Toots went up the ladder and over the eaves with the weekend supplements to the *Los Angeles Times*.

Karen's attention span ran out, or what is more likely, her mind filled up with Nola in about an hour. "I'm going down to find Nola for paddle tennis," she announced between putting on her tank top and lacing up her sneakers. "Do either of you two want to tag long? Sue? Toots?" No answer. Toots crossed her front feet and looked small. "OK. Sue, will you watch out for the dog?" Sue nodded, so Karen took her paddle and vanished.

Heat and internal chemistry caught up with Sue about the time she finished the book reviews. It was probably crash-out time, so she removed her front-upper dental bridge for comfort, slipped it into the side pocket of her shorts for safe keeping, and zonked out for a while. When she awoke it was with the undeniable feeling she had been invaded. Toots was lying alert with her legs crossed, which allayed her fears that someone might have sneaked into the house. Thinking to go down for more tea, and wishing to be presentable, she naturally reached into her pocket for her front-upper dental plate and came up with...nothing!

Panic, undiluted!

She shook the towel, shook the papers, shook her pants, shook herself. Anticipating a body-search, Toots stood and shook herself. "Toots! You didn't!" In a genuine fright, Sue stormed down the ladder, into the house and into Karen's room where Toots' bed was kept, her bed where she took anything she thought interesting. There she found two incisors and bits of pink plastic, a suggestion of upper-front dental work, but not even enough left over to glue together.

Sue's bitter crying had more or less stopped by the time Karen and Nola got back, so they got the story with few dramatics. "Toots ate your teeth?" asked Karen. "I think you two are the only ones in the world this could happen to. What this is going to cost me, I'll be a long time taking out of your hide, Toots."

Nola whistled at Toots, who went over and sat between her knees. "You just hide in there, while I tell these dumb clucks all about my free dentist."

"The Venice Free Clinic! Of Course!" said Karen. Sue's mood brightened. "I sure can't make a living looking like this! Shit! I can't even leave the house!" To everyone's credit, they all got the giggles.

"There's usually a waiting period of several days, but maybe I can get you a dispensation from Dr. Chung."

Early the next morning, Monday, Nola called Dr. Chung. An hour later he was looking into Sue's mouth holding two wet x-rays in his hand. "I see three teeth here that could possibly be saved..." Life drained from Sue's miserable being. "...so there's nothing we can do for you here." Sue began planning her suicide. "So I have taken the liberty of making an appointment for you at the Department at UCLA. Nola, can you go in with her, right now? I imagine they will want to pull teeth."

Nola nodded; Sue nodded, as if her assent really mattered in this scheme of things.

"Take her to the head of the department. He's waiting for you." The head of the department found Dr. Hans Karge, a graduating senior who needed to do multiple extractions (the very idea made Sue tremble) and full upper and lower plates in order to graduate.

You have to give Nola credit. She stayed with Sue the whole day, through making the molds, all the novocain injections, the blood and the stink of extracting all but three of Sue's teeth. Nola hung in there holding a hand or two and talking, nearly fainting herself but still there. When it was finished, she delivered Sue home and put her to bed with the downer Dr. Karge gave her.

While the swelling subsided Sue tanned and read on the roof, far from the ridicule of cruel but well-meaning friends. There is something about being toothless that puts you in immediate contact with your own old age and mortality. Immanent conditions which you are advised to first face alone, if you have the choice. By week's end the temporary plates were ready, and Sue came out of isolation, which she passed off as a "vacation." Everyone thought she looked wonderful, but no one recognized her teeth as being new. Within the next two weeks she had her 'permanent' false teeth which were prettier than ever.

After her last trip to Dr. Karge, Sue smiled her broad new smile at Karen. "Hold out your hand, Little Karen." Karen did, and saw twenty cleaned and sparkling gold inlays fall into it. "For the elves," said Sue.

Chapter 17

While Karen cleaned up the kitchen, Sue located one of the recent billmies and settled in the bath tub. She had just settled into a warm bubble bath when the telephone began to ring. Since rushing was out of the question, she acquiesced as Karen picked it up and reported, "It's Jorge on the phone from downstairs. He wants a couple of nice turquoise rings for his girl. Can you go down there with a tray of rings? He wants me for advice, too."

Sue knew better than to keep a customer waiting too long. "Tell him I'll be right there." She quickly dried off and dressed in shorts and shirt.

Jorge and his girl were waiting for them in the living room. The shades were pulled, and there was a conspicuous and slightly ominous pile of black cases on a table in back of the couch. Jorge took the two ring trays from Sue. "Oh, these are really nice! Here, honey," he said to his girl, "See which ones you like, while I dicker with Sue."

He turned his attention. "What I'd like to do is a trade," he said, directly if uncertain. "It goes like this. Behind us is a pile of five guitars, four electrics, one classical, all hot, and I've got to get them out of here! You see, Mom has this crazy friend who steals things and gives them to the people he likes. Somehow he ripped off these instruments from a rock band on tour, staying in Santa Monica. I can't go to them or to the cops to give them back. We'd have the cops all over this place, and considering Mom's reputation as a fence for big ticket stolen stuff, someone would end up in jail. Mom has so much stuff stashed here I don't even have room for the guitars. Can you imagine if the cops started looking around? And I can't sit here any longer with the shades pulled, or the cops will have suspicions enough for a warrant. So will you give me a couple of rings for them?"

"Sure!" said Sue. "Karen and I can unload them at the swap meet. Karen, do you have enough other stuff yet?"

"I can go swapping any old weekend. This time of year the best place is the flea market in Saugus."

"Have you found a couple of rings, honey?" Jorge asked, and then said to Sue, "Here's the plan. Drive the hearse through the alley and stop by the gate. Open the side door, and Karen and I'll run out the back door with the cases. Now, go." And she went.

Approximately two minutes later they were driving down West Washington with William Randolph bulging with hot guitars. "Now what in hell do we do?" moaned Sue.

"To my garage!" commanded Karen, "the one I rent to keep my swap meet stuff. We'll load up now and go to Saugus early tomorrow."

For once they let everyone else go in to Hollywood on a Saturday night without them, and turned in early. By seven o'clock the next morning they had driven up to Canyon Country, to the Saugus swap meet and had set up their three church chairs and two collapsible tables, one with four sizes of T-shirts and the other with Sue's jewelry trays.

Sue was on the way from the hearse with two guitars, the reason for the whole trip, when Karen stopped her in her tracks. "One at a time, man! You don't want the cops to notice too much, or they'll start checking serial numbers."

She chose the classical guitar for the first time noticing it had a beautiful tone. She had no sooner opened the case than the swap meet gates opened for the buyers. Two men were onto the guitar immediately, obviously having come to the swap meet for a guitar. "Make me an offer," suggested Sue, who had no clear idea of the value of stringed instruments.

"Will you take a hundred, plus this new set of golf clubs?"

Karen, the athlete, undressed one of the heads and played around with the club. "Beautiful clubs! Brand new!"

"How about one-fifty and the clubs?" said Sue.

"Sold!"

Well, they got three for the clubs, two-fifty for each of the Fender electrics, and left for home with almost fifteen! Sue handed the whole roll to Karen. "Here's your half plus mine, to cover the stash Rat Bart stole from you a while ago."

"That's way too much," said Karen. "Here. Take back three. Wow! Now I can finally get that beautiful International Travelall I've been looking at!"

"As for me, I'm out of breath!" said Sue as they pulled out of their parking slot and headed back to Venice in time to go to the beach.

Taco and Nola
—Rooky of the Year and Most Valuable Player

Chapter 18

Sue heard Danny and Juice whispering at the door and let them into her workshop before they knocked. "Let's keep the noise down, and go into my bedroom. Let's not disturb Karen and Sylvia."

"BIG Sylvia. An amazing arrangement," said Danny. "I guess we can hold a meeting of the abduction committee with a quorum of three. Can we use your phone, long distance to Frisco?"

"Juice, you go bring the phone in here while I get us all some coffee. Maybe my mind and body will be awake and engaged by then." By the time Sue got back, her two guests had finished their phone call and were looking glum and staring at the phone.

Danny was speechless, but not Juice. "I told you Bart would never give back Karen's stash and never come and take me back. My crummy brother can't stand me around any more than I can stand him. Since you guys kidnapped me, he got used to not keeping an eye on me, and not having to watch his language and which girls he was fucking. So you may as well just relax and let me stay here in Venice with you. Besides, when Charles moves up north I'll be the only one left at Highland House who can cook. I do most of it now, anyway."

"You've got something there, kid." Danny put the phone on the floor. "I guess you can stay, but you can't just lump around like the rest of us flakes."

"What else is there, besides softball and paddle tennis and dope and sex? You guys never take me anywhere anymore."

"We do too take you places, whenever it doesn't matter that you're jail bait. Don't lay a guilt trip on me about that."

"But I look older than I am."

"You may look sixteen, but you'll never pass for eighteen. But don't change the subject. You've got to do something constructive, like go to High School."

"I can't stand going to high school! Ugh!"

At that point Sue was ready with a compromise. "So don'y go to hight school. Go to Santa Monica City College already."

"I thought I had to graduate to go there."

"They take high school seniors, if their grades are good enough. If you want a high school diploma next spring, you can take the equivalency test."

"My grades were good. What's this equivalency test?"

"If you pass it, you get your diploma. If you were my kid, which you kind of are, you'd take the Scholastic Aptitude Test, too. Goldie Glitters can tell you all about it. He goes to SMCC. You could even take the bus down and find out for yourself what you need to do."

By that time Juice was getting enthusiastic. "Goldie was home-coming queen last year, wasn't he? It must be a pretty good place."

"And another thing, what are you going to do for money?" Danny wondered. "Tuition is free. There's always food and a roof with me, but what about clothes and books and stuff?"

"You mean...get a JOB?"

"Now there's a novel idea," said Sue. "What can you do?"

"Besides sleep around?"

"Besides. Like, can you type?"

"Sixty-five words a minute."

"Wow! I think that makes you one of the high-skilled among us! If you're willing to work for the minimum, I think you could get a part-time job pretty easily." Danny almost sounded as if she had some acquaintance with the working world.

"Hmm...," Sue mused. "Now that I have teeth again I need to rewrite my resume so I can look for work. If I can get a hold of an IBM Selectric, can you do the typing for me?"

"As a matter of fact," Juice confessed, "I am, shall we say, 'acquainted' with the girl who runs a duplicating service on Saturdays. Believe me, she would be glad to have me banging her Selectric early some weekend morning."

"You're hired. How about doing term papers and reports for school kids? You could put an ad in the newspaper, too."

"With money in my pocket.... Do you think they have any pretty girls at SMCC?"

"Maybe one or two," teased Sue.

Danny, who had been staring at her feet, looked squarely into Sue's eyes. "I thought you were making a good thing of the jewelry business."

"Yes and no," Sue responded. "The market isn't what it used to be; frankly, the business is beginning to bore me."

"You wouldn't really think of selling yourself to the establishment again, would you, Sue?"

For the first time Sue saw a sadness, a lost look which she could neither ignore nor allow. "Why Danny Mae!" she said. "I think you're suffering the empty nest syndrome!"

"And I thought I wasn't cut out for motherhood!"

When her two early-morning clients had left happily for home, Sue washed and stacked the coffee cups, feeling as if all was right with her world. Optimism lasted only as long as it took Flor to hike over from Highland House and climb the stairs.

"Oh, I'm so glad you're home," Flor said without knocking. "Can I come in?"

"Flor! Of course, honey. How do you take your coffee?"

"A little milk, please." They settled in Sue's shop with the radio down very low.

There was a peaceful softness in Flor which made Sue, seeing through Kimmey's eyes, almost fall in love. "You don't often get over this way. How have you been? And how's Evelyn these days?"

"That's just it. Evelyn's fine, but I'm not. Anymore." Flor had that relieved but disturbed look.

"I gather you and Evelyn are having problems."

"Everything was wonderful at first," Flor began. "I was really happy, at last marrying out of the barrio and all. But then the money ran out, first Evelyn's Unemployment and then my bank account. I expected her to do something for us, but all she did was lie around the shack and smile a lot, and play softball once a week.

"Sounds like a case of no confidence to look for a job," said Sue.

"Worse yet she can't do anything anyone would pay her for. So I did what every chicana does when there's no money in the house, clean the Anglos' houses. Evelyn came along on the jobs, and now we even get contracts to clean and paint rental properties for the realtors."

"That's what I call hard work," said Sue.

"Tell me all about it! Then Evelyn took up dealing, but she doesn't have the nerve. All she does is smoke and stay home all day. I do all the hard work alone.I think she is plain lazy."

What Flor needed was some quick answers, but Sue had more questions than answers. "Jesus! You are in a hard place! What are you going to do, Flor?"

"At least my brothers knew how to deal, and there was usually food and a roof. Honest, Sue, I'd be better off back in the barrio keeping house for my brothers and hustling a little on the side."

"Don't do anything drastic yet. Have you talked to Danny?"

"No. I came right to you, because Danny is Evelyn's special friend, and I don't want to put her in a bad position. Evelyn's so nice, I hate to be complaining about her this way."

"Sometimes a little grumbling can help you feel better about everything." Sue was surprised at her own clinical approach to disaster in her friends' lives. "We could do worse than have a family conference," she suggested.

Flor nodded and smiled for the first time that morning. "It's worth considering." Then, as an ominous afterthought she added, "I wonder when Kim is coming to town." If Flor felt better, Sue felt worse.

Chapter 19

"Yoo whoo! Sue!"

Kimmey's shouts raced ahead of her up the stairs, through the bead curtain, and into the bathroom where Sue was soaking her deserving body. "I'm happy," Sue said from the depths of bath oil and bubbles, "that no one else has the nerve to talk to me that way. Come in and keep me company while I get the last of these barnacles."

Before Sue could object, Kim had taken the invitation literally, was stripped and sitting in the other end of the loaded tub. "How long has it been since you shaved your legs?" Sue asked.

"Never," said Kim indignantly. "How about yourself?"

"Roughly six years. Amazing isn't it, how much people resemble chimps from the knees down. What brings you out and around so soon after beach time?"

"Well." Kim settled into the suds. "Singer called."

"You mean *Singer* Singer?"

"Yeah," Kimmey crooned. "Oh, yeah. There are four tickets to her concert waiting at the box office."

Sue rolled her eyes back. "Manna from heaven! And I'll bet you're going to take Flor."

"Sure, and you'll take Nola?"

"I see what you mean. Is it that obvious?"

"So who's watching? Since none of that can happen, why don't we make it a stag party? Silver has gone to East El Lay on the bus, so Danny is on the loose. What about Karen?"

"Shazam!" came Karen's voice from the sunroom.

"Strange, isn't it," said Sue, "how some cases of rock and roll deafness go into remission under the right circumstances?"

"Some kind of miracle cure," Kim agreed. "Danny Mae split after breakfast, but she'll be back about six o'clock."

"We better leave Highland House by six-thirty. Pull the plug, if you can find it, and let's get dry."

Before Sue could honk the horn on the hearse Danny appeared from nowhere wearing her field boots, a red and black wool shirt with a pair of Charles' Vietnam camouflages and carrying a small, compact back-pack. She stuck her head in the window on the driver's side just as Sue remarked, "I don't understand your outfit. We're going to a concert, not on a bivouac!"

Danny pulled her fedora down to mid-forehead. "You can never be too sure. We'd better go in my Porsche for a change."

Sue parked the hearse and Danny pulled the ancient Porsche into the street. Its fundamental military green was blotched with auto body primer soothing the multiple eruptions of parking lot pox. Gangrenous rear lights wore prosthetic red cellophane taped over remnants of busted glass. The whole top of the car had been amputated and a roll bar welded in place.

"Danny never wants to drive. I wonder what this is about?" Karen said.

"Damned if I know, but I'm just as pleased to be a passenger for a change," said Sue.

"Even if we're down-graded from cabin class to steerage?" Kim looked with distrust at the Porsche.

Unsure, Kim dropped into the co-pilot's seat. Karen and Sue, being the smallest and the shortest, went over the side into the sparse rear seat. "Keep an eye on my pack, will you, Sue? I can't leave such a huge stash at home alone, and can't deliver it for another couple of days." Danny requested. Sue felt around with her feet, and sure enough, there was the back-pack on the floor. Danny buttoned up the collar of her shirt, pulled her fedora down so tightly the brim touched her steel-rimmed glasses, and they all settled in for a windy trip.

They got to the Forum in plenty of time for Kim to pick up the tickets at the box office, and still had a leisurely half an hour before it was time to get to their seats. As they strolled back to the Forum, Sue hooked her arm through Kim's and gave it a little squeeze. Kim looked down at her with a smile that was less truth than bold-faced hope. "I'll be OK, pal. I've been to these things before and didn't get a heart attack."

"You've got guts. I never know how I'll react to old affairs."

"I'll let you know when it's time to leave."

The show began. Singer, the image of hopeful youth, stepped off the covers of her earlier albums. In the unforgiving stage lights she was no longer merely pretty but positively beautiful, no longer just inspiring but electrifying. When the message was complete, Sue didn't feel quite so alone in her disgust with the war in Vietnam.

They stayed through the new songs and the old songs to the very end, and even took Singer's invitation to champagne at the motel afterward.

It was a small party, a rarity for Singer. The base guitar tended the door, maintaining a quorum of about six fans as they stopped by for autographs and friendly banter. The female lead guitar settled into one corner and played softly while Karen fell in love with her. Kim and Singer lounged around on the bed with her agent between them, in charge of decorum and the champagne bottle. Sue pulled up a chair and they all talked about war and peace and freedom.

Meanwhile, Danny found a corner to hide in, squatting on the floor with her back against the wall and the back-pack clutched between her knees. The longer she hunkered there the more threatened she looked, and the faster her blue eyes, behind her steel-rimmed glasses and under the brim of her hat, darted left and right. Her face was grim to the point of fear.

Eventually Singer noticed the spectral Danny. "Kimmey, what about that lumberjack you brought with you?"

"Oh, that's Danny Mae. She's completely harmless."

It was nearly three o'clock by the time the party quit and the Venusians headed for the parking lot. "You're sure you can drive OK?" Kim asked Danny.

"I'm cool," Danny answered.

"Then no one will mind if I hang out here for a while," Kim said, and disappeared back inside.

That was the last Sue heard before she collapsed in the back seat, done in by champagne and narcolepsy. In twenty minutes

130

Danny dropped Sue and Karen at their apartment on Rialto street. Too sleepy to stumble upstairs, Sue crawled into William Randolph's corpse door and rolled up in her sleeping bag for the rest of the night.

Sue awoke to a familiar sound—tennis shoes running in place beside the rear fender. "Kimmey!" she shouted, throwing open the corpse door.

"Like old times, eh what old pal?" Kim handed Sue two dixie cups of fresh coffee from the Germans, and inserted the new Singer tape into the slot in the dashboard. Sweet guitar and sweeter song filled the morning as Kim settled back into the jump seat and commanded, "Hail the conquering hero!"

"Damn," said Sue into her coffee, "I knew I shouldn't let you stay there alone. And you were counting on me."

Kim chuckled. "But you were zonked out. Besides Singer had a yen for a roll-around with the old Kim, and that's all there was to that." It seems I can get that one into the sack any time I want. What I can't stand is competing with the entire civilized world—so I won't."

"But where does that leave you?" ask the worried Sue."

"In love with Flor."

"So what else is new?"

Chapter 20

Karen, Toots and Sue were the last to arrive, taking up the last two places at the table. When her little bunch of indentured slaves brought themselves to order, Danny rose to make the announcement. "The mescaline is here!"

Everyone oo-ed and ahh-ed as she set out five one-kilo bricks of stuff that looked more or less like wheat flour. Beside that stack she placed thirty boxes, one of which she opened to show a thousand green gelatin capsules.

"I figure," Danny continued, "if we start now, in a month we can put all of this into all of those. At a buck a hit wholesale, which I have firm orders for in the Bay area, we'll have enough money to give Charles his equity in Highland H 8.Äouse. He wants to buy that boarded up bar next to the Germans. And I can pay off the whole damn mortgage on the house."

"Far fuckin' out!" said Karen.

"Free and clear?" asked Flor.

"All thirty thousand?" Nola asked.

"Man, that's a lot of work!" said Evelyn.

"It won't get any less if we just sit here looking at it," said Sue.

Interpreting these remarks to be assent, Silver put out a stack of dinner plates, a roll of waxed paper. Danny opened the first kilo of mescaline. "Take one scoop from the open ki onto the plate. Put the plate on a sheet of waxed paper so you can pick up what gets spilled. OK? Go!"

Every hour or so everyone took a break for beer or grass or whatever. That regimen worked perfectly until the end of their fourth hour. When they stopped and looked up from their work, their heads rolled back, and they kept right on rolling until everyone fell back into their chairs as high as they could get from breathing the mescaline. As soon as Danny was thinking again, she got Charles in from the garden and sent him to Sears for some of those white paper dust-masks the machinists wear. The second day's shift was a full eight hours.

By month's end there were sixty ZipLock baggies of five hundred green barrel capsules each. "How big is the air filter on William Randolph's carburetor?" Danny wanted to know.

"Oh, about this big around and that tall," Sue said with help from her hands. "You wouldn't! Oh, yes you would, wouldn't you! I guess if we took out the filter and oil...."

Danny nodded and looked at the ceiling. "I've got three hundred bucks for gas to the peace march in Seattle—by way of Maude's Bar in San Francisco, naturally. While I do a little heavy dealing in Richmond, the rest of you can play around for a day in and around San Fran. Then we can drive on up the coast to the Peace March. Can William hold together?"

"Oh, could we, Sue?" Flor begged through her Sophia Loren smile which she knew Sue could never resist. "I've never been much of anywhere, you know."

In the exhilaration and chatter Silver took Danny out onto the back porch for a quiet deliberation. "I can't go to San Francisco."

"Why in hell not? We'll have a great time."

"I just can't go. I always get into it up there. Last time I went to jail, and I'm not up for that again so soon. Besides, it's been a long time since you were out to howl without me hanging on. I can go in to see my brothers with a load of mescaline."

"OK, if that's how you want it, but who's going to keep me out of trouble?"

Having won her point Silver chided, "Knowing you that could be a problem. Take the dog, Ruby. Stay close to the hearse. You'll stay out of jail."

Danny re-organized all the chickens into a flock to make plans. "This time it's a stag party," Danny insisted. "Last trip, you couples always wanted to set up camp early, and never wanted to play in town. So Flor and Evelyn, you decide which one of you is going. I think the hearse can hold all the rest of us. How about tomorrow morning?"

"Sure," Sue agreed.

"Shazam!" said Karen.

"I'll call both my jobs," Nola said with the phone tucked between her ear and shoulder. "Will a week be enough?"

"Man, you guys are really up for this peace thing! Maybe I should get the TV fixed when we get back."

That from Danny was all Flor's sensibilities could stand. "Aw, Danny. Do you have to? I got so tired of the body count and watching all the shooting."

"She's got a point," said Sue. "You can count on me to tell you when the war is over, and in the meantime, if anyone gets curious you can come over and listen to my TV."

"Listen?" said Danny.

"Yeah, listen to it. The tube burned out about six months ago, and anyway I only had it on when I was making jewelry, which precludes watching."

"What do you think, Sue," said Danny, "should we be doing more for the anti-war effort?"

Sue lapsed into her philosophical mode. "We all registered to vote Peace and Freedom. I do plan to vote against the fucking war. We all do what it comes to us to do. What we do best is exercise our freedom. We go to jail for being nude. We deal clean dope which isn't going to kill anybody. Above all we're out of the closet, which could turn out to be dangerous. As for the Peace March, "I've given that question considerable thought. I've been to a few marches. It's one way to say we don't like the war. People seem to get some satisfaction. It couldn't hurt to go."

Wild cheers.

While the room buzzed with talk of sleeping bags and telephone numbers, Flor and Evelyn retired to argue it out in the garden shack. Eventually Flor returned, so happy she didn't dare think beyond anticipating the sauna and cold shower in Stinson Beach.

"OK, everybody!" shouted Danny, loud enough to re-establish order in the prevailing enthusiasm. "Take along one of the green pills. Drop it before breakfast tomorrow, and we'll trip through the whole trip to Maude's Bar!" Aside to Sue she said, "I've got two rolls of those little mini-bennies that work so well."

With the last gulp of her orange juice, Sue dropped two of the new bennies. By the time she had gassed up William Randolph she herself was nicely gassed for the trip. At Highland House she honked and waited for her five passengers to emerge. And there they came, as alike as the pills they had dropped. Each wore a Fedora, sun glasses, and denim flight jacket. "Did you guys plan this?" Sue asked.

"Nope," said Danny, shaking her head. "It's the wisdom of mescaline."

"At least you can all vouch for the uniformity of the mixture and the dose," Sue said.

"All together, everybody," said Danny.

All together, the five Venusians filed aboard through the coffin door.

Eight hours later they filed back out again, and found themselves standing at the curb in front of Maude's Bar. "How in hell did we get here?" asked the bewildered Danny.

"Some kind of space warp?" suggested Sue, just before she crashed out for her usual.

The party was well under way by the time Sue, awake again and in command of her wits, had pulled on a clean T-shirt, combed up a little, and re-joined the mob in Maude's. Sitting side by side at the bar, and eating from identical boxes of egg rolls from the Chinese restaurant next door, were her five friends.

At the end of the row sat Patty (the Wicked Witch of the North) cozying up to Juice, of all people. Fully comprehending the disgusting implications of that arrangement, Sue stood riveted to the floor until she heard Danny hailing from the back of the bar, next to the men's crapper.

"Hey, Sue! Come on over here!" Sitting on the stool next to Danny was a small but energetic woman with short hair, flushed cheeks and star-spangled blue eyes. "Meet Mo, until recently Sister Francis of a teaching order in Saint Paul."

"Glad to meet you, Sister."

"Call me plain Mo, and God bless." She was drinking red wine with a doughnut on the side, enough like sacrament to be disturbing. "I hope you don't mind if I take Danny home with me tonight." With that, plain Mo disappeared into the crapper.

"I hate to be a kill-joy, but..." Sue slid up on the stool and hung a foot on the rail. "...I don't feel right letting you go with someone we don't know. Anything can happen to you, no matter what kind of street smarts you've got."

"A nun?" queried Danny Mae. "What can happen, hey?"

"Remember the Inquisition, or did your Jewishness insulate you from that dark episode in Christian history? Don't underestimate the kinkiness possible in the clergy."

"If I pray to Saint Joanie?" She was grasping at straws.

"A fat lot of good her prayers did her, and she was talking into powerful ears."

"Ruby can come with me. How about that?" Danny finished her beer and plunked the glass on the bar with an air of finality which Sue recognized as impenetrable.

So she gave up. "That sounds more like it. I can't imagine Ruby letting anything rotten go down. Now tell me what I can do, without you, about that," she said, throwing a thumb in the direction of the table at which Patty had relocated herself and Juice.

"That arrangement scares the shit out of me too. Juice and Patty are probably going to shoot up together and I can't do anything about it. I lost control over Juice when she discovered sex, and I sure can't influence Patty at all. I don't know what to do, and I think you should give up, too. I'll meet you back here tomorrow night, or in Stinson a lot earlier." With her fedora on her head and Sister Whoever on her arm, Danny strode out of Maude's into a night fraught with dangers only an atheist could imagine.

Not resigning easily, Sue hollered after her, "I wish Kim had a phone out there. I could at least call out the Maa-fia if you need us." For once she ordered up an Irish coffee hoping the alcohol would live up to its wide reputation.

"What's this? Real booze?" Nola clucked accusingly as she

136

threw a long leg over the stool Danny had just left, and settled in next to Sue.

"I thought Yaz might be hanging out here on a Saturday, but I guess not," said Sue, sadly dwizzling her hot drink.

"That's right," Nola replied. "You've got something like a big thing for Yaz. She's not here."

"Last time I saw her she wasn't speaking to me. I think she has someone else. I'd better forget about her. This trip north has gone south, man. I can't keep this flock of skittery chickens together anymore."

"Well, here goes another one. I'm going home with Nancy."

"For once," said Sue, "I have no objection."

"For once, I've found the one dyke in California with a steady, full-time job."

"Do me a favor. Drive the hearse out to Stinson? Flor doesn't drive very well, and I'm so tired I'll fall asleep."

"Sure. We can follow Nancy. You can zee all the way."

Sue crawled into her sleeping bag after her bennies wore off and before Maude's closed. When she came to again the hearse was in Nancy's driveway with its engine running, and Flor was leaning through the partition. "Wake up, Sue. It's time to drive us over to Kimmey's."

Slowly Sue established contact with the world, and then slipped out the corpse door and into the driver's seat for the rest of the trip.

The hearse moved so deliberately and slowly they could hear every turn and lump between Nancy's driveway and Kimmey's gate. Some might say it was the late hour, but Sue knew this slow pace was a controlled reaction to the contact high of heightened sensibilities that made her want to hurry before Flor simply exploded from anticipation. At last they were there. Flor slipped out of the passenger's seat, opened wide the tall wooden fence, and quietly closed it behind the hearse.

The sleep-drenched figure of Kimmey pushed back the curtain and turned on the porch light. Still unable to see to the outside, or possibly not believing what she saw there, she opened the door a crack. There in the headlights, illuminated like a miracle in a bolt from heaven, stood Flor, alone. In one

137

smooth motion, like the second hand passing midnight, Kim in her boxer shorts went over the railing and across the gravel to the cool patch of grass where Flor was waiting in the headlight beams. As they stood in each other's arms there was room for nothing between them but their tears of pure joy.

If it had been only a case of mere love, or even sex, Sue would not have been too embarrassed to watch. As often as she had seen her many friends hug and kiss each other, nothing had seemed so completely personal and nearly intrusive to watch as Kim and Flor's joy in one another. In humility, Sue switched off the headlights and left them wrapped in merciful darkness.

Eventually their tears would wash away their months of hopeless longing, and they would be able to speak and move like normal people again.

Sue unfurled her sleeping bag on the water bed at the far end of the wooden deck. As she searched the cold clean stars she wondered where Yaz was on a night like that, but lacked the courage to walk down the hill and knock on her door. Narcissus and Goldman, at last grown to young cats, whirred themselves to sleep, one in each armpit. Their softness was of some comfort to Sue's broken heart.

In the leaden morning slightly before the mauve of daylight, Sue felt someone lay out a sleeping bag and roll in beside her. When Narcissus and Goldman returned purring, she rightly assumed her mattress-mate was friendly and she crashed back to sleep.

"Is that you, Sue?" came a creaking voice beside her.

"Danny Mae? I thought you were doing that nun on Frederick Street."

"Shit. The nun." Danny buried her face in her knees for a moment before starting the story. "I stopped at William Randolph for my sleeping bag and my dog and a box of kibbles, and also picked up a couple of hits of mescaline."

"You mean, you opened up the hood and the air cleaner, and exposed thirty thousand dollars worth of dope to the full view of every snoopy eye on Cole Street?"

"Ninety thousand, retail," Danny corrected. "It wasn't as if I had taken down my pants. Taking your car apart on the street is no big thing in that neighborhood. Anyhow, Plain Mo had her car, so we went to her place over in the Castro, which she shares with two gay social-psych grad students from Berkeley.

"As soon as we got inside, the roommates wandered by...for introductions, I was led to believe. Pretty soon we went into her room, which didn't have any doors. Every ten minutes or so, one of the guys wandered by on his way to the kitchen.

"We weren't quite so visible when we moved onto the bed. I was getting comfortable, so I made conversation. 'How long have you been out of the nunnery?' I asked.

"So she says, 'Two months. Now that I'm finally out I want to exude warmth, so I got a pet until I find a steady lover.'

"So I looked where she was pointing and saw this forlorn blue bird in his cage all alone. Now, some people swear by birds, but I can't see anything warm about them. So I thumped Ruby on her chest and said, 'If you want a really warm pet to exude warmth with, get yourself a nice, big old dog.'

"'Dogs eat too much and they have to go on walks,' she said. At that point the blue bird looked not only forlorn but bored. 'I think you should at least get the bird some toys,' I said.

'Oh, he has toys,' she said. 'He has a frisbee and a rubber lamb chop.'

"That was the last straw for old Ruby. She jumped up on the bed and plunked right in between us. If you believe in non-verbal communication, Ruby was shouting something about male psychologists watching through holes in the wall. So I took my sleeping bag and my dog to the highway, and you know the rest. I wish I had brought Silver along. I think she keeps me out of more shit than I can imagine."

The nine o'clock sun and a rapping sports car engine raised a vocal response, a grim rumble, from deep in Danny's sleeping bag. "We better stay asleep until Patty splits."

"Patty and the Ferrari! Of course. Who else drives anything that sounds like that?" Sue zipped the cover tighter over her head.

"If that other voice I hear is who I think it is, we'll have Juice to bring down."

"Juice! I'll drop this house on Patty if she has messed up our little mascot."

"I'm with you, Dorothy, but not until I'm straight." Danny zippered in so tight the world turned to mumbles. That meant there were two of them sealed and insulated from what happened next. All they heard was the kitchen door banging open, a deadly 'plud' of metal against wood, and a seismic shaking of the deck and house.

Curiosity overcame their fear. Sue and Danny each opened her sleeping bag just enough for a look in the direction of the 'plud.' What they saw was an axe, with it's blade buried in the door-frame and its red handle still vibrating from the blow. "Does that thing belong there?" Danny whispered with her eyes as wide as can covers.

Sue whispered back, "That thing is Kim's Girl Scout axe, and it belongs on a hook in the living room, beside the Franklin stove."

Kim's voice rose to a high, angry pitch. "And I'm going to leave the axe right where I flung it, to remind you never again to mess up any of my nice friends, especially Juice."

Next came the rattle of fancy boots across the gravel, and the near-terminal rap of the Ferrari fleeing toward Mount Tam.

When they felt the water bed shaking they opened their sleeping bags and saw Kim's bare foot pumping it up and down for attention. "Can I get you to put Juice to bed on the couch? Juice wandered onto the deck, nodding off on her feet and looking as if she had been punched in both eyes. I'm too busy to see to Juice myself. And I don't notice either of you guys volunteering."

Danny rubbed her eyes and shook her head. "She's more than I could manage with this barrel of mescaline floating around my brain."

"Did Patty see Flor?" asked Sue.

That about straightened Danny out. "Flor!? Is she in there, too? So that's what this is all about!"

"She's still waiting for me in my loft." Kim said as she wandered through the kitchen door and climbed back up the ladder.

Sue stretched out her nakedness on the wooden deck warmed in the Pacific sunset. "If we leave within the next hour we can be in Richmond in time for dinner with Leland and your main customer...."

"Slow up, man. It will take another two days to get our Venice gang back together, even if we can find Karen. Where the heck is Karen, anyway?" Danny asked.

"She's in San Raphael with a lady deputy sheriff."

"So," Danny continued. "Add a day to find Karen, three days drive to Seattle, and the peace march is over with before we get there." Danny sighed. "Oh well, I guess we do well to keep everyone together, fed and housed and alive—these days."

"So we might as well do a sauna and shower."

"And leave for home on...say, Sunday?"

"Monday night."

"And get home in time for the beach on Tuesday."

In all that time Yaz was nowhere to be found.

Kim and Windsong

141

Chapter 21

Nola wasn't just lucky; mainly she was parsimonious. Her bred-in-the-bone cheapness that found every day on the way through the sand between the surf and Ocean Front Walk enough 'deposit' pop bottles to buy a fresh pack of cigarettes.

In addition, she was a gifted 'trasher', with a sharp eye out always for good clothing and treasures for all of her friends. Whenever possible she drove through alleys behind small factories where the surplus was dumped. In back of a leather jacket company she found twenty pounds of leather, neatly boxed, and useful for patching jeans. A similar box was underneath, with chamois trimmings, from which Sue stitched a pair of pants.

Basically, Nola knew a good thing when she saw it. Her crowning achievement was the discovery of Windsong lying around Venice beach with a contingent from Maude's Bar in San Francisco

Windsong was a trim, healthy, well-maintained young woman of mostly Great Plains Indian heritage, on the breathtaking side of attractive. No doubt about it, she was worth looking at; but she was also worth watching and listening to. To her, all of life was guerrilla theater. Everything she did was equal parts drama and political content, drawing on her special genius for ethnic English and body languages.

She was an easy success as a teacher in San Francisco's alternative school, where they put all the smart but troubled minority kids. She maintained discipline by loving ridicule, moving easily between ghetto swagger and barrio shuffle. With Windsong behind them, her students made silk purses out of the sow's ears of their lives. Everyone loved Windsong, and everyone was right.

Windsong rode into town with Phyllis and Priscilla, folded up in the luggage space back of the seats in their molding MG Midget. Looking for the rays, like any sensible San Franciscan, they went immediately to the beach where Sue was staked out for browning with the rest of the unemployed gays and lesbians. Almost as soon as they got there Windsong dropped her beach umbrella and landed on the unsuspecting Sue, kissed her expansively and ground the both of them into the sand. "Sue, you old chingadera! You really came down to Angel Town? And I thought the Stinson Farewell was just an excuse for a party!"

"It was worth moving south for a reunion like this," said Sue, wiping sand off her vital places. "So where's Molly?"

"At home, grumbling. Hang onto my beach towel while I wash all the sweat off the bod. Then we'll get caught up." Off Windsong ran to the ocean.

Nola, who had watched this madness, managed to speak. "Who was that? You've been holding out on me, you old dog."

"Calm down, Nola. I'm nothing to this one. I gather she is recently available, though."

"I'm paralyzed! How am I going to ask her out?"

"I think you'll find some way," said Sue.

"Thea will kill me."

"She'll be hurt, but surely she's too good-natured to be dangerous."

"That's what you think! I get black eyes if anyone even looks at me. When I do what I feel like, there'll be blood."

Then Windsong was back, flopping wet on her towel. "Windsong, this is Nola, and vice versa," said Sue just before she escaped to the sea.

As usual on beach days, Sue arrived late and, on the way down to the water, searched gay beach for Nola's surfboard sticking up out of the sand. But it wasn't there. "Has anyone seen Nola?" she asked anyone who cared to answer.

"Well," answered Gary, "not in person, but I did see a green Econoline van with a beat-up surfboard on top, parked in front of the Royal Inn."

Eventually two female figures inched their way toward the water's edge, almost too involved with one another to manage their loads of beach blankets and umbrellas, sand chairs and a cooler of drinks and sandwiches. Where she used to arrive with only a towel, its edge stuffed under her belt, Nola was suddenly burdened by an overdose of her own internal chemistry and the nearness of Windsong.

No one remembered seeing or hearing from Windsong and Nola until Nola called Sue on Farm night, always on a Wednesday. "*Please* say you'll come with us," Nola pleaded. "I *know* the Farm is a men's disco, but they always accept women on Wednesdays and they have the best records in town. And no one cares if we dance close. We always have a good time there, don't we? Besides, it's the only place Thea doesn't go."

"When you put it that way, what can I do? With me and you and Windsong at the same table, she might not suspect, if she comes in." Sue had to laugh out loud. "Who are we kidding, anyway? My being around might slow her down, though."

So it was arranged. Anticipating that Nola might not be capable of proper attention to traffic and other matters pertinent to driving they went in William Randolph with Sue at the wheel.

She picked up Nola and Windsong at the Royal Inn where Windsong was staying and where Nola had been hiding all week. When they were sitting side-by-side in the driver's cab, Sue pushed in the new Carly Simon tape and opened the windows to let the summer jasmine breeze assault their sensibilities. Considerably calmed by the nearness of friends and soothed by the salves to her raw nerves, Nola's confidence in her safety allowed her to extract her straight-edge razor from inside her boot and lock it up in the glove compartment.

They all had a good time dancing and watching the men watch each other. Before the place got really packed, about midnight, they filtered toward the back door on the way out. As they passed the dance floor Sue whispered "Duck, you guys!" which Nola and Windsong did. "I thought I saw Thea in the incoming crowd." When they thought it might be safe again Nola stuck her head up like a tall hunter in a short duck blind. Whatever it was had vanished, and the matter was forgotten. They drove back to the beach and called it a night.

When Sue got home the lights were all out on Rialto Street, and a light summer breeze riffled through the curtains. She quietly tip-toed to her own room, shed her clothes into a relaxed pile on the floor and settled onto the cool sheets. She had no sooner heaved the heavy sigh of approaching sleep when the phone rang.

"Hello?" Sue said softly into the black hand-set.

"Sue, this is Nola. I'm at Thea's."

"Thea's!" Sue exclaimed in a high, squeaky whisper. She closed the door, sat firmly on the edge of her bed and demanded to know, "What the hell is going on?"

"She was waiting outside the room when we got to the Royal Inn. I didn't want Windsong to get involved, so I went along with her, and now the whole thing has gone rotten. I'll tell you when I see you. Can you come and get me out of here, quick? I'm really scared of what I'll do."

"If you'll pardon my partisan interest, I'm more concerned about what Thea will do. I'm on my way."

On the way in to Hollywood Sue remembered the straight edge razor, and dove into the glove compartment. It was still there. Was that good, or was that bad? Before she resolved the question, she was there, parked and running down the walk to the cottage at the end of the court.

As soon as Sue rang the bell, Nola was there. By the bright moonlight Sue could see the blood on Nola's face, her sopping shirt front and sleeves reddened from her elbows to her hands. "It's not as bad as it looks," said Nola.

"I hope you're right," said Sue, "because it looks bad from over here."

"She gave me a bloody nose, and I wiped it off on my sleeves."

"Let's go back to my place so I can wash your shirt. Otherwise you'll scare the shit out of Windsong."

"Yeah," agreed Nola. "She not as tough as she sounds."

"Why couldn't you stop Thea?" Sue asked.

"I usually hit her back just with an open hand, but it was closing and I couldn't trust what I'd do."

"So you got hurt yourself instead." Sue could only shake her head.

The next day Windsong went home to San Francisco, but was back the next weekend and the next and the next. During each week Nola saw as much of her Venice pals as usual. One Wednesday morning, while she waited for Karen to get home from a mid-week foray to Sylvia's in L.A., Nola settled on the mohair chair like some giant migratory bird with her long arms, like tired wings, wrapped around her knees. "What I need," she said with a sigh, "is a nest." For a while she savored that idea and continued, "A nest of my own, I mean. Every place I go belongs to someone else, and I have to do everything someone else's way."

"What's the matter with your van?" Sue asked. "It seems to me living in your van is the very style that already lets you have everything your way. If you don't like it one way, you immediately park the green van somewhere else. You're not telling me the whole story."

"All right. What I can't have in my van is a weekend guest."

"So! You're in love!" ventured Sue. "I would guess...Miss Royal Inn?"

"Yeah, Windsong," drawled Nola, as close as she could come to saying 'Shucks.' "I've always been in other people's homes, but I don't know how to find a good place for myself. Will you help?"

"Sure," Sue said not really sure at all what she was agreeing to. "I can keep an eye out." This seemed more like a job for Danny, but Sue was in for it now.

"But for god's sake don't tell Karen!"

"Karen will disown you for keeping a secret like this. Besides, she'll have to know sometime."

"Sure, but in the meantime I don't want to hear her trying to talk me out of it and running down Windsong. What can a person do when a friend starts going for you? Did you know, she still nearly has a fit when anyone else plays paddle tennis with me?"

"It's just one of the hazards of lesbian life," said Sue "But with Karen, multiple attachments seem to be a way of life."

Weeks went by. No apartment seemed right to be Nola's place. Finally, early on a Thursday, she came by without her paddle tennis racket and tossed sand at Sue's window. "I've got it!" she whispered. "Come down alone, without Karen."

Sue tippie-toed down the stairs in her bare feet, and laced up her tennies as the van rolled through Venice. "Tell me about it."

"It's Steffie's place, over the garage."

"Steffie the speed freak? What have you got yourself into?"

"For better or for worse, I paid two months in advance. And now we've got to fix the place up. Come on, I'll show you."

The place could only have been the product of a genius speed freak. Part of a wall had two coats of red enamel over white, left unfinished because the can dried up, and resumed some time later with still another color. Every wall had been decorated with the same dwindling decisiveness. Where paint splattered on the floor it was spread thin with the brush so it dried quicker. Taped to the refrigerator were two classified ads from the Venice Beach Head: "Speed makes your tits shrink," and "FRISBEE LESSONS: Is there anything better to do?"

"This ambiance couldn't be costing you over ninety dollars a month."

"Seventy. Utilities paid."

"As my aged second mother-in-law is fond of saying, 'Anything worth ten cents costs ten cents.'"

"Where do we start?"

"Any place will do."

Pictures and posters had been cut out with a small pair of scissors and stapled to the wall. Where one staple would have sufficed, at least ten had been pushed into the margins. Sue spent a busy hour prying up staples and peeling off pictures while Nola went for buckets, mops, brushes, sponges and cleaners of several types. Beginning in the kitchen, they scrubbed down the whole place, finishing up with a good hosing. They left the place open to blow- and drip-dry overnight.

The next morning over doughnuts they debated color. "I don't know how you feel," said Sue. "But in my days as a real estate fixer-upper fixer, I would never use anything but Antique White. It goes with anything else, so you can wait until later to decide on the furniture."

"Yeah, I like white, for walls. I'm tired of dark places with heavy black curtains, where you have to light candles all the time. I want to open all the windows and let in the sun. You know how I feel about the sun. And look! I have a view of the ocean!"

It took two full and tiring days to paint the place and scrape up the variegated colors from the floor and from the windows. Finally it was time for a day-long tour of the second hand stores. For a song (maybe two songs) Nola got two thicknesses of antique white lace-and-net curtains. A couple of dollars more got them a set of satin sheets far beyond any reasonable dream.

From somewhere Sapho snagged a comfortable double bed with bed spread, and a carefully used nine by twelve oriental rug. Nigel, bless his heart, kicked in with a set of three Edwardian boudoir chairs. From the Goodwill came kitchen—and dining-ware and a set of Kennedy rubber duckies for the oversized bath. Millstein's General Store had three affordable Art Nouveau pictures.

When the tough work was finished, they settled on the floor to survey Nola's new world. "If this is my own place, I guess I can have my own rules, can't I?" asked Nola. Sue nodded gravely. "Rule One: No Smoking."

Sue waited for The Big One—What else would Nola outlaw? Flirtations...beer...? But it never came. She put the cigarette pack back in her pocket. "OK! Maybe we can all quit yet. How will we recognize each other in the dark without our smoker's hacks?"

It remained only for Nola to hang her shirts and patched jeans next to her softball uniform on the closet rods, lay out her shorts in the top drawer of the bureau just above her collection of size large socks, and meet Windsong's plane on Friday PM.

Saturday AM Nola dialed her new white phone and got Sue on the line at the precise time Nola would usually have been playing paddle tennis with Karen. "I want to thank you," said Nola, "for your part in creating my new life, by inviting you to have Peruvian dinner with me and Windsong tonight."

Sue had not eaten out after dark (except for breakfast after the bars closed) since her penultimate paycheck in Illinois. But since this was Nola's treat, Sue allowed herself complete enjoyment of the tasty fare and fine California wine. After finishing her coffee, she excused herself to go to the Ladies' at the back of the restaurant.

When she came back no one was at the table. The check was gone, so she hurried toward the front door, angry with them for making her run to catch up with them. As she stepped over the doorstep there came a strong grip on her shoulder and a snarl in her ears: "Don't even think of leaving without paying!" It was the manager.

"Neither of those two women paid?"

"Pay up, or I'm calling the cops!"

What else could she do?

When Sue finally got outside, the two other women were in the van, Nola starting the engine and Windsong urging her to get a move on. "What do you two mean, skipping out like that?" Sue asked.

"Whatever do you mean? Would I do a thing like that?" Windsong chirped.

"How do you like that? First she skips out. Then she sticks me with the check, and then denies the whole thing! And where were you going so fast? Ditching me?"

"You didn't pay, I hope," said Windsong.

"See here: Dine and dash doesn't work here in Venice; not if you hope to live here."

With the advent of Windsong, Sue hoped her softball responsibilities were relieved. "I know the whole game bores you," Nola admitted, "but say you'll come along anyway, to keep Windsong company."

"But she can't stand me. How can I be very good company if she can't stand me?" Sue wanted to know.

"She can too stand you! I mean, she does too like you!"

"Then why did she stick me with that check on that dine and

149

dash escapade? I think that whole episode expressed her opinion of me."

"You mean, she never paid you for that check? She said she did."

"No, she didn't. Damn! I didn't want to mention that. That mean trick, all that denial and trying to get you to ditch me didn't work. You and I are still pals, and...."

"Please come along to the game with us anyway? You know we always have fun at that bar afterwards," pleaded Nola, who didn't care to know any more.

"When you put it that way, OK."

So the strange three-some went to the game. After Nola parked the van at the park, she took herself, her mask and her mitt into the dugout for warm-up.

"I'm starving," said Windsong, cool but civil. "Can we get a burrito anywhere around here?"

Sue was relieved at Windsong's willingness to talk to her at all. "As a matter of fact, about a block from here they make a white-hot green-chili stringy-meat burrito that will change your concept of cholo." With these and a couple of large cokes they kept themselves occupied while everyone got organized for the game.

Their preoccupation with food precluded conversation long enough for Taco to arrive, the heroine on crutches, to bask in her fame as a base-stealer. Several times she stopped to let her fans sign their names on the leg cast acquired the afternoon she stole home.

With considerable effort she got on her pins, crossed the green and climbed into the bleachers. Then the sound of Windsong's voice boomed across the stands: "Hey, look! It's Taco!"

Taco gave a shrill whistle through her teeth.

"Come on, Taco! Come on over here and sit next to me!" The two of them joked around and hugged all through the game.

Finally softball was over. When the game moved to the bar, Windsong grabbed Nola on one arm, Taco on the other. There they sat, the three of them, with Windsong the center of a dyke sandwich where she really liked to be.

But it didn't last long. As soon as her cast was removed, Taco got a better position, all-day every-day 'helping' Jan and Dee run the burger stand. Jan and Taco ran the front of the business, rang up the cash register, took the orders and delivered them to the customers. Naturally there was a good deal of horse-play which Dee watched while she cooked alone back in the kitchen. Within the month the name of the place changed to 'Dee's Burgers,' Jan was back selling life insurance, and she and Taco were installed in their own apartment.

What Taco did better than steal 'Home', was steal home and hearth.

Chapter 22

"News" is only what you can bear to hear. Everything else goes unnoticed and unreported. That Cherry was going to have a baby everyone knew and could grasp as acceptable in some way to his or her mentality. But allowing Cherry to be pregnant would be to allow a 'father' to 'impregnate' her in a process inimical to the local frame of mind. Consequently, as Cherry got bigger and bigger, more and more ungainly, she was noticed less and less, to the point of virtual invisibility.

From time to time Cherry had to confirm her own reality. On those days she stopped to see Sue who, alone in their circle of friends, had had the misfortune to fall in love with a string of heterosexual women and was thereby more or less familiar with the process. In return for a serving of tea and visibility she did Sue's tarot and filled in her own supply of silver pendants to re-sell to her mystical trade. "Did you know," Cherry asked Sue, "that your pendants are magical?"

"I try," said Sue. "I spent several days in the library finding just the right shapes with just the right meanings, but it took a while to get straight on the colors of the inlaid stones. Remember the batch with the male colors on the female signs?"

"That was pretty funny, a product for limited clientele. For a greenhorn you've come a long way, honey. I hear it from everyone. Your pendants really do have magical power. Remember that first moon-and-stars I got? It keeps getting lost and finding itself again. You are what we in the trade call a 'source', whether you believe in mystical power or not. What have you got for childbirth? It could happen next week."

"So soon?" Sue thought a moment. "I think the best thing you can have with you is Katherine."

"Harumph! I'm not counting much on her! Jerry will probably show up, though, and even if he doesn't, I'll be OK because I was wearing one of your moon-and-stars at the time of conception."

The next week word went out that Cherry and Katherine had twin girls. In whatever number, whether delivered by a doctor, midwife, Parcel Post or any other sterile agent, babies are cause for celebration.

Gary got together a baby shower, at his new and sunny apartment. Being it was an afternoon occasion everyone agreed to dress out as they had for the wedding of Evelyn and Flor. What kind of presents to get seemed to stump everyone but Sue. With a little jaw-boning and arm-twisting she arranged for a good supply of disposable diapers, some small under-shirts, even more six-months' shirts and some one-year cover. Sue herself brought two pairs of one-year blue jeans.

When the wine had been drunk, the grass all smoked and the downers downed, it was time for the naming contest, after which the babies were Athena and Helen. Finally Cherry and Danny, stood looking at the two small but very curly heads. "But your hair is so straight, Cherry! Does curly hair run in Katherine's family?"

Cherry did a double-take. "Think what you're saying, Danny!"

Several months later Katherine and Cherry moved out of the big house they couldn't afford and still support twin toddlers. When Sue stopped in to see them in their under-sized apartment, Cherry was out for the afternoon at a feminist awareness seminar leaving Katherine to watch over Athena and Helen who chewed on her overall cuffs.

Katherine popped one of the beers Sue brought, sat with her elbows on her knees and shared the latest news. "Well, our happy home is on the skids. The kids are going to live with their father, and Cherry is going up to the Susan B. Anthony Coven in Marin County." Finally she shook her head and mused, "You know, Sue, I was never cut out for fatherhood."

"And Cherry is a better feminist mystic than a mother. What's this I hear about a play Cherry is in, at the down-town

153

Women's Center?" Sue asked.

"Anything you might have heard is probably true. Z Budapest wrote it, and you know how the Los Angeles press flocks whenever that intelligent , sexy, lesbian mystic comes out of hiding. If I were you I wouldn't miss it."

The occcasion of the play was Winter Solstice. Everywoman, in the person of Oak Woman from the Feminist Wicca was looking for a child to assist in the ceremonies of awakening the world. Each of the Middle Eastern Gods offered to provide a suitable child. Allah looked around the burning desert but failed to find a child.

Jehova, in the person of Cherry, had been snooping around in human affairs, and thought he knew how to do it. He recruited the virgin Mary, who was as new to the business as he. He ordered her to lie on the ground and performed a brief set of pushups over her supine form. She soon protested, and he was exhausted anyway. "How does Man do it. He makes it look so easy."

Everywoman was desperate. The Goddess, in the person of Z saved the day. "You should have come to me first. Every December I have this new year's kid hanging around. So babysit a while and have your party." One of Cherry's twins toddled on to the stage and everyone, cast and audience, celebrated Winter Solslice.

Chapter 23

"If I didn't have a going jewelry business, or if they gave me more than forty dollars a week maybe I wouldn't resent this quite so much every time." Sue said one morning.

"Maybe it's getting up this early," grumbled Little Karen into her morning coffee.

"But we're always up this early."

"It has something to do with standing in line."

"Yes," Sue agreed. "And holding out your hand. Furthermore, it disrupts our lives having to go in there every two weeks. If it's true we worked for this money, why do they make it feel so much like welfare?"

"They should send our Unemployment checks by mail."

When their biweekly encounter with Unemployment was all over, the two women celebrated with omelets at the Germans' while they waited for Nola and her tennis paddle. "You two even smell rich," Nola said as she slid onto her chair. "Now we can go to the Baja."

"Mexico?" exclaimed Sue.

"I don't have to show up at Unemployment for another eight days, so I can get out of town safely," Nola explained.

"It's been years since I've been to Mexico," said Sue.

"Count me out," said Karen. "I'm going to L.A. with Sylvia, as usual."

"Then I'll have to talk Sue into this all by myself."

At that point Kimmey and Windsong entered in a general swirl and settled. "All ready to go?" asked Kim, looking directly at Sue.

155

Sue laughed. "I think you guys rehearsed all this!"

"Of course," Nola admitted. "What I haven't mentioned is that we're all going in the hearse."

"What's the matter with your van? This whole thing is your idea, after all."

"I don't want to put all those miles on my van," Nola admitted.

"What a cheapskate!"

"And besides," said Kim, "We can't see out of the thing. I never could understand a van with no windows."

"Well, OK. I feel like I've been had somehow, but OK."

"You'll be glad," said Kim. "Yaz is going, too!"

With her heart on her sleeve and money in her pocket, Sue loaded her friends into William Randolph. A reluctant Karen sat in the window of her sun room, piping them out of town with a chorus of *Dardanella* on her soprano saxophone. Yaz, in a blacker funk than ever, hid in the back of the hearse behind a pile of sleeping bags.

Nola would say they terrorized the Baja, and Nola would be right. But there was no trouble in Tiajuana. Culture shock confined them all to hiding in the hearse long enough to blast through town with no beer stops.

At the south end of town Sue abruptly pulled into the parking lot at the Flamingo Nite Club. "Beer time!" Nola declared. But as soon as the four trucks behind them passed and went onward, Sue pulled the hearse across the road into a Pemex gas station.

The mob was speechless, wonderstruck at Sue's linguistic ability as she negotiated for a full tank of gas in Spanish. "How come you know this lingo?" asked Kimmey with considerable admiration.

"If you live in Los Angeles long enough, you just naturally catch some of it...."

"Like some throat disease?" asked Windsong.

"Or infectious hepatitis?" offered Kimmey. "I'd like to arrange to catch a little Spanish from Flor the same way I caught hepatitis from—"

"We know, Kimmey, we know!" said Sue, laughing. "As for you, Windsong, you could do with a good dose of Spanish, if you ever hope to teach in Los Angeles."

"Hrumph," grumbled Windsong. "I guess they aren't smart enough to have learned a little English by now."

Kim got the strangest look on her face. "Wow, that's what I call a weird attitude coming from an Indian."

Something in Sue needed to de-fuse the situation. "I didn't think I could ever learn enough Spanish to be much use to me," said Sue, laughing. "But then when I drove to work, I started listening to Elenita Salinas, morning D.J. on radio station KWKW. Forty minutes every morning of that sweet, soothing Mexican voice had to ease a few nice phrases into my mind."

So far, so good. Somehow Sue transported her carload of urban refugees to Ensenada, and they escaped into a Mexican community which she believed to be safely bilingual. Bilingual they were, safe they were not. The Mexican men, who had only recently made the jump into accepting pedal-pushers, weren't at all ready for the Venice uniform of tank tops, cut-off jeans, buck knives and tattoos.

"Please try to stay together, you guys! If anyone gets too far behind it would be too easy to get lost, and then what would we do?" It was too late already. Windsong was already half a block away, with Nola running to catch up. Kim and Yaz, those cool and easy souls, poked around the stores quietly, the one always smiling, the other always polite. Leaving Kim and Yaz to look at abalone and silver rings, Sue ran forward to find Nola and Windsong.

You could hear Windsong all over the store. "Twenty bucks for this frigging cardboard Mariachi hat? That's four times what it's worth!" Not willing to fork over even five bucks, she and Nola ran out in a huff.

In the interest of international tranquillity, Sue stayed behind to soothe the temper of the store manager. By that time Team one was catching up and Team two was on the move and ducked into another shop. Where Sue's linguistic skills might have been of some use, she spent most of her time barking at their heels and urging them into a contiguous group as if she were a sheep dog.

As the group ran through the streets they collected a crowd running along with them and wondering where the fire was or the burglary.

The septet of amazon Norteñas stormed the restaurant on the Ensenada pier, and stuffed themselves on a lunch of lobster. Notoriety, which had preceded them from shop to shop in town, finally overcame Windsong, student of guerrilla theater and ex-urban brat. She went wild, called for the manager, and refused to pay her bill on the grounds that the food was rotten.

"What," queried the manager, who was at least as tough as Windsong, "is so rotten about the half of the food left on your plate, and so good about the half you ate?"

The literacy of his English as well as his impeccable logic stunned Windsong. "Well, I'm just not going to pay, that's all," she retorted in a huff.

"Then I'm going for the police," said the righteous manager, already on his feet.

"Hold on a minute," said Sue with a hand gentling his arm. Turning to Windsong she continued. "If they take you to jail, as they certainly will, no amount of talk on your part will keep you out, and no amount of bail will get you out before the trial. You'll be stuck in a Mexican jail, which isn't near as homey as American jails. There's no public defender and you'll be in for fraud, a very long time."

"Then it's time somebody fought their lousy system!"

"That's Mexican business," said Nola. "If you want to go to jail for your rights, you can do that later when we get home. Now, apologize and pay up. And hope he forgets the police."

Windsong grumbled a lot but with Nola twisting her arm behind her back she paid up so they could all pile back into the hearse. "*Now* is it beer time?" pleaded poor, dry Nola.

Mindful of Nola's recent contribution to peace and international tranquillity, Sue ignored her better judgment and relented. "*Now* it's beer time!" she announced. With her heart in her mouth, and saying a desperate prayer to the Mayan god, Qetzalcoatl, she rolled William Randolph past all the tourist traps to her favorite parking place next to the alley back of Hoosong's Bar.

"Everybody out!" Kimmey ordered as she opened the coffin door at the back of the "bus." The swarm of desperate dykes flew out onto the sidewalk, buzzed around the corner and collected inside Hoosong's Bar, where a crowd of male American tourists were more than ready for them. By the time they had settled at a long table at the back of the place one of the men had arranged a round of Hoosong's famous margaritas.

It was too late already. The dust-thirsty women tossed down half a glass, waited until their eyes returned to their sockets, and finished the rest. With minimal effort Nola snagged a waiter and ordered up another round.

Confident that this was her last moment to minister to her own thirst, Sue slipped up to the bar and ordered a large coke. She had been settled back into her own chair for several minutes when she realized Nola was gone. "Where's Nola?" she asked no one in particular. In all the noise Kim could only gesture with her thumb thrust in the direction of the Ladies' Room.

Sue pushed the door open. No Nola. She glanced back to the table. No Nola. Then she ran out the back door, into the alley, terrified by the darkness and the evil implicit. There was Nola, surrounded by a determined group of American men, all urging and coercing her toward the door open into their Winnebago camper.

Sue was powerless. She stepped back into the bar and hollered "Kimmey!" Kim heard, rose out of her chair, wiped her sweaty palms on her haunches, came running and stopped abruptly when she got the picture.

"She's going for it?" asked Kim.

"So far only jaw-boning," Sue summarized.

"Whoa! That one's trying to push her into the camper! Next, fucked meat!"

"Shit!" said Sue. "OK. Ignore those guys, pretend they don't exist. Stick close to me and make as much noise as you can. We'll run in there, grab her, and run her out to the hearse."

"*GO!*"

Miracles! Kim grabbed one arm, Sue the other. With all that energy coming their way, and not accustomed to being ignored, the knot of men parted like the Red Sea. The girls ran Nola through that mob of muscle, around the corner and in through the coffin door.

"WHA…!" Nola was open-mouthed.

Kim looked her square in the eyes. "You were gonna be their gang-bang." Nola crumbled and passed out.

Sue went back for the other women. Not looking forward to keeping this tribe out of trouble, Sue elected to corral them for the weekend in a nearby camping compound full of American families.

At the Licores they put in two cases of beer and a couple of packs of Cokes, all at room temperature but only Sue seemed to care. Anticipating their wants, the American owner of the campground had plenty of shaved ice to fill their coolers.

As soon as they found a parking place at a safe distance from the rest of the campers Sue sent everyone out looking for firewood. She busied herself carving up a barracuda purchased from an enterprising fisherman. Soon they had a good dinner and a fire to huddle around. Her only disappointment was that Yaz was always some where other than by her side.

"I think I'm being avoided," Sue complained to Kim. "What's the matter with that woman? Better yet, what's the matter with me?"

"Well, you have to make a little effort after all."

"Watch this, if you don't believe me." As soon as she stood and headed for Yaz's side of the fire, Yaz moved some place else. In this case she settled in with Kim which finished the discussion as well as the evening.

Breakfast was a dozen eggs, scrambled on the Coleman stove and a dozen fresh rolls from the bakery down the road. That, and cups of instant coffee, held everyone until noon when they swarmed back from the beach wondering what's for lunch.

Sue was feeling like head camp counselor. "Well, if we're going home today, we should go within the hour, and eat somewhere on the way to the border. In that case I'm going to have to throw away the last half of this lid of grass we've been smoking. I'd never get it back across the border. Besides, I'd feel silly

160

smuggling American home-grown."

Nola, the cheapskate, settled the matter. "Why don't we get another fish like the one we had last night, and cook the grass with it for lunch?"

"We still have beer," Kim observed. "We'll just stay until we sober up."

It was twenty-four hours before anyone could move again. Sue drove slowly and carefully back to Tiajuana with all the windows open to the ocean air, and a tape-full of mariachis playing on the sound systems. As they rolled into town Nola's mind engaged. "Let's stop for liquor!"

"But we'll never get away with it," said Kim. "The border fuzz will go through this hearse like a dose of salts. Isn't that true, Sue?"

Sue nodded gravely. "They'll never throw us in jail, but they can pour all the booze down the drain. Could any of you watch that without crying?"

No one answered immediately. Finally Nola spoke up again. "I'm going to try it anyway." That did it. By the time they were in the line leading to the border there were ten fifths of liquor rattling around. "Where can we hide all this?" Nola asked. The answer came without voice: Between the sleeping bags which had all been rolled out in the back. Nola smoothed out two bags and laid the bottles end to end down the center of the floor from front to back. On each side of the row of bottles she laid out a sleeping bag to keep them from rolling around and put another heavy sleeping bag over the whole assembly.

When they pulled up to the kiosk the border guard took command. "Everyone out, and take your suitcases with you. Driver, stay in the car while I go through it." In two minutes flat everyone was searched and back in the car.

"They didn't find it?" asked Kim.

"They must be idiots!" Nola announced.

"Would you all look at this?" Windsong was laughing as she felt along the top of the layers of sleeping bags. "Nola stashed all the bottles in one long line under here. The border fuzz must have thought he was feeling the drive shaft cover!"

They awarded Nola the Nobel prize and all settled back for a

161

moment. "What a trip!" said Nola. "I think we should do this once every month from now on."

Sue had not expected such an early chance to speak her mind. "This trip has not been one I would care to repeat any time soon. Nola, it took both me and Kim to get you out of the hospital. It is only by sheerest luck Windsong is still out of jail. I wish you two would watch it a little, and stay off the sauce."

"We're really sorry about all that," said Windsong.

Nola put her arms around Windsong, smiled into her bright brown eyes and said, "Honey, do you think that woman is trying to tell us something?"

Chapter 24

Sue sat propped against William Randolph's steering wheel enjoying the next to the last Coke from the cooler watching her friends collapse. They were exhausted piles of people in the back, rising and falling with every breath, mumbling and sinking into well-earned sleep. All except Kim who hunched in the co-pilot's seat looking unhappy. Seeing that, Sue continued sounding off. "As for you, Kim, you're a knight in shining armor, a tower of power when I need you."

"Then why do I crumble so fast when Patty shows up?"

Sue sighed and shook her head. "I don't know, kid. What do you get from her— besides horse?"

"Hmm. Besides horse. Well, after we shoot up until I'm strung out, she leaves me all alone at Stinson with a wad of traveler's checks, two more cases of noodle soup and enough junk to get off again. Then she pays another few months on the mortgage and goes back to the city. Eventually one of her finks tells on me, that I'm healthy and chasing around, and she chases me down."

"And that's it?"

"Sure. What else do you want?" said Kim.

"How about a little vegetable-beef soup for a change? How about a little sex. I mean, you could have sex."

"We haven't done that for some time."

"Let me get this straight. You let her destroy you in order for you to be acceptable, and then she lets you down, denies you a little affection?"

Kim nodded, said gravely, "That's about it. The story of my life," curled up and drifted off to sleep.

Sue took the two remaining bennies with the last swallow of Coke in the can hoping the combination would get her to Venice. Once again, and for the last time, she counted noses. Then she laughed and whispered softly to herself, "What a carload of dependency problems!"

Several hours later the automotive sounds changed and Kim stirred from deep sleep with her mind engaged. "Tell me again, Sue. What's a dependency problem?"

Sue's foggy mind unloaded through a leather mouth. "The dependency problem," she croaked, "is more like a question. Who is going to take care of me?"

"Oh yeah. In my case it's who's gonna buy the vegetable-beef soup." At that point a traffic light turned red and Kim recognized the end of the Nixon Freeway. "You mean you drove all the way back from Ensenada? And you didn't fall asleep?"

"Two mini-bennies go a long way." When she was used to the sound of her own voice Sue continued. "I couldn't say this to anyone else...but at the moment I'm driving through a maze of red spider webs, so I'm about at the end of my rope."

"Any sign of the monkey walking the center line?"

"None. It looks like I'll last long enough to deliver everyone home."

Kim fished around in the slush at the bottom of the cooler and the dust of the glove compartment. "One Coke al tiempo and a dried up Pall Mall. Breakfast for two."

A few blocks later Sue stopped the hearse at Nola's nest, and the weaving figures of Nola and Windsong made their way up the cement steps. Under way again toward Highland House, Sue drove down Main Street. As they rounded the traffic circle, Kimmey whistled and Sue honked at Karen and Sylvia walking hand in hand.

Awakened by all the racket, Yaz looked out the window of the corpse door just in time to see Karen and Sylvia waving and whistling furiously. She snapped to attention, opened the glass to the driver's cab and asked sleepily, "Who's that with Karen?"

"That's Big Sylvia, Karen's lover," Kim explained. "I guess you've never met her."

"I certainly would know if I had," said Yaz through a giggle.

Sue explained further. "My guess is they have just come from their usual Saturday night at Sylvia's place in L.A., had a spot of breakfast at the Germans', and are on the way to Rialto Street for a quickie before beach time."

"The very idea of that combination is inspiring," said Kim.

"B-b-b-but Sue," Yaz interjected. "You and Karen are living together! Aren't you two an item?"

Sue and Kim stared at each other as the light bulbs of comprehension went off in their heads. "An item? Certainly not!" said Sue.

Kim howled with laughter. "Well, I guess that explains a few things."

"More than a few," Yaz agreed. "Like the way I left you high and dry that evening of the pizza over the carrousel..."

"...and the way you vanished from Stinson the weekend of we didn't go to the peace march..."

"...and the way you kept running away from poor old Sue, the whole damn trip to Mexico," said Kim.

Sue was so stunned by reality and excited by the implied possibility that she was near to passing out in a narcoleptic seizure. Nevertheless, she managed to drive around the corner to Highland House and let Kim fall out onto the grass. "How about a ride to the Bacchanal tonight?" Kim asked.

"Sure. Look for me about nine o'clock," said Sue through an accumulating mental fog.

Yaz slid into the passenger's seat and moved in close to Sue. "We had better get you into the back before you pass out. Go on along without me, Kim. I'm sticking around here for a while."

The sun was up and warm at Sue's back but she avoided crashing until she made it into the back of the hearse face down in Mexican sand. The last she heard was Yaz's sweet voice saying "You just leave it all up to the old Yaz."

Some time later Sue was aroused by a rain of tennis balls on William's tin roof. The Carole King album played softly on the stereo speakers, and in the background the balmy surf swirled around in the drenched sand of a high tide. Furthermore her shirt was open, Yaz was dozing with her face there, and...something interesting was going on in her genital region. All of this pleasantry was the usual content of her hallucinations upon awakening from a narcoleptic sleep. She thought nothing more of it except to keep her eyes closed in order to enjoy her hallucinatory sensations a little bit longer.

Then she smelled it, Chinese incense! Hallucinations never included olfactory stuff! Sue snapped her eyes open and found she was surrounded by Yazmina! "Where did you find the Chinese?" she asked as she moved her arms around Yaz to keep her a while.

"In the cabinet over the driver's cab."

"Then I'm not hallucinating after all?"

"We're parked back of the paddle tennis courts down at the beach. I closed all the curtains, so you just lie there and enjoy, while you catch up with me." She was kissing Sue under the ears while hastily opening the placket on her cut-offs.

"Oof!" Sue responded quickly. "You don't understand. When I wake up from one of these things I'm usually ready to go!"

"I guess I have a lot to learn about you. Do you think we should get naked now?"

"Let's not mess with non-essentials," Sue said as she rolled Yazmina onto the Mexican sand, kissed her soft Persian mouth and made way under her tank top and into her swimming trunks.

From then on neither could tell who did what and what happened to whom. Too soon they lay there sweaty and drained.

"Honey," said Yaz, "can we learn to make it last a little?"

"With practice, my love, with practice." They wrapped around each other and dozed until sunset.

After an early meat loaf special at the Germans', Sue and Yaz stumbled up the stairs to the Rialto Street residence just as Karen and Sylvia were hanging out the wet stuff from the beach.

From the vantage of the roof, Karen did the introductions. "Sylvia, this is Yazmina."

"Hi Sylvia. I've heard a lot about you." said Yaz in the understatement of the year.

166

"May we have the bath room for a while?" Sue asked.

"Shazam!" said Karen.

"Try some of my new lilac bath and body oils," Sylvia offered.

While the water ran in the tub, Sue and Yaz took their time about each other's clothes, finally standing on them and holding each other close. Detecting a certain slump in Yazmina's demeanor, Sue commanded, "Into the tub before we let it overflow!"

Once they were settled side by side in the large square tub, Yaz soaped up the soft cloth and eased the sand from Sue's back, specially attending to her underarms, breasts and tummy button. "Now," said Sue, "come over here and sit between my legs with your back to me."

"Is this a good idea?" Yaz wondered as she settled against the accommodating upholstery of Sue's eager frame.

"I think it's a terrific idea." With great care she sudsed Yaz's neck and face and torso with the soft cloth. "I like you slippery," she said. With even greater care she let her bare fingers check around the folds of her lover's genital region.

Yaz responded by raising one knee and letting it fall outward, coming to rest on the side of the tub. "Jeez, Sue! Don't ever do anything like this unless you mean it."

"Well I do mean it, so I guess we better get out of here and dry off, unless you prefer to finish up in cold water."

In record time they were out, dried, wrapped in towels and standing in Sue's studio. Quietly she locked the door behind them. "Now!" she said as she threw both towels in the corner and took Yaz to the clean, cool sheets.

It was wonderful lying there toe to toe, mounds to mounds and mouth to mouth. There was plenty of Yaz to grab hold of, from her strong upper arms, down her back to her firm, white Persian buttocks.

Unobtrusively, almost shyly, she moved to admit Sue's hand to where it was already slippery. "Jeez, Sue, you make me feel good! There! There! How did you know all this?"

"It takes one to know one."

"For god's sake don't stop!"

"Certainly not. Not until you say." Sue couldn't help laughing at all the verbage. "I think your speech center is connected to your genitalia. Quiet."

Yazmina let herself be loved until the long slow rolls culminated in that one strong push. With her ears still ringing she lay heavy in Sue's arms.

Eventually their minds engaged again. "I wonder why it took you and me so long to get together?" Yaz mused out loud.

"What was I to do? You wouldn't even dance with me at Maude's for the longest time," Sue complained.

"At first I thought you and Kim were doing a number."

"There's a lot of love between me and Kim, but we're just pals. We never came close to a sexual arrangement."

"I didn't want to interfere where my friends were concerned," Yaz explained.

"And I thought you didn't like me."

"Not like you? I just love you, Sue. You're so sweet and considerate. I think I'll take you home to meet my folks."

"You know who's going to be pleased is my sister!"

"Will you listen to us? We're the two squarest people in Venice!"

Chapter 25

Promptly at nine o'clock Sue honked in back of Highland House, and Kim, in undisguised depression, shuffled out and sluffed into the front seat with Sue and Yaz. Momentarily cheered by her friends' pleasure in each other's company, she heaved a mock sigh of relief. "I don't believe it! You two have weathered the whole day without some crazy misunderstanding?"

"Thanks to you we got everything squared away," announced Yaz.

"Well, it took you long enough. Could it be that congrats are in order, after all your tap-dancing?" teased Kim. "Hey. What's that I smell?"

"Lilac," said Sue.

"You've been rolling in the lilacs." Suddenly Kim slipped back into her previous despond. "Seeing you two so pleased with yourselves does the old Kim a lot of good, but shit, man! I've had about all I can stand of Highland House with Evelyn and Flor all over each other, and then on top of that there was the little matter of the front tires."

"On the Ferrari?" asked Sue. "Again?"

"There it was, kneeling down on its rims, a two-inch slice in each tire, and what do you mean, again?"

"Didn't you know? It happened the weekend of the wedding, if you'll pardon the expression. Patty ordered up two new Michelins before you two left, that morning at my place."

"Is that a fact? Why didn't she tell me? All of a sudden I don't understand anything." Kim sat quietly contemplating her new view of the situation. "The thought of bruises I can handle, even broken bone, but a person can die from knives, and the bitch didn't even tell me!"

As they sat there in the alley talking and collecting themselves, a splatter of Italian invective, dressed in white jacket and pants, flew by them and into the house.

"Shit!" shouted Kim. "It's Patty!"

"Silver will kill her!" Sue answered.

"And Juice is there! Patty will be out after Juice again! Help me, you guys, we gotta take this thing apart!"

The verbal part of the battle was on when they stormed in.

"Bitch, get out of my house! You dirty everything you touch," Danny screamed. Silver advanced out of the kitchen, where she had been cooking, with a knife still in hand. "It's OK, Silver. She's too far beneath you to bother damaging her."

Patty sneered at Danny. "Silver, huh. If my name was Gold, would you like me any better?"

At that point Kim hollered "Come on, Juice. We're getting you outta here." She grabbed Juice by one hand, and since Juice had hold of Yazmina by the other, they all flew out of there in one long string. They were out of the house, in the hearse and gone before anyone knew they were serious.

By the time they were on the freeway Kim and Yaz were packed on the front seat with Sue while Juice was relaxing on the jump seat in back. "Argle barg!" Kim growled, just loud enough to be heard. After an extended contemplation she announced, "I've completely lost control of my life."

"Oh I don't know about that," Sue said. "It seemed to me you directed that last scene fairly well, to say the least."

Unconvinced, Kim said wistfully, "I wish...I wish we were in Stinson and could take a sauna and cold shower."

"You're not seriously suggesting we hit the highway, I hope." Sue assumed an open posture. "But I warn you, if you insist only a little you'll find I'm a pushover for almost anything to make you smile."

After some minutes of silence and an extended search of her pockets Kim finally came out with it. "Why don't we look up Patty's connection in Hollywood, for a nice piece of hash for you two love birds and a few hits of heroin for me?"

Sue was livid. "So now you shoot up when Patty isn't even in sight? You self-destruct, whenever you so much as think about the Wicked Witch? I call that complete surrender. OK, let's do a really good job of it; if we turn on and then go blasting around town, I think we could arrange to be in jail in half an hour."

"But damn it! I have to do something to get rid of all this anger and all this lovesickness and jealousy."

"If you two want to get good and drunk, I promise to stay sober to do the driving," Yaz offered.

"Well," said Kim. "It's too hot to turn on, anyway." Off they went to Nola's back bar at the Bacchanal.

The manager recognized need and desperation when he saw it in old patrons, and let them in without a cover charge. Ski, the band leader, was there wearing her white jeans and whiter cowboy shirt, banging the cowbell while her band gave out all the rock classics.

Nola had seen her Maa-fiosa through the crowd, and had free drinks ready for Kim and Sue and Yaz when they settled at last around the corner from the service bar. "Are we all alive and moving?" asked Nola, "or are we part of one of Sue's dreams?"

"I think we're still high from Mexico," said Kim through a laugh which Sue was glad to hear. The therapy was working for the moment.

It was Nola's break-time. She slipped through the slot in the service bar and stood between Sue and Yaz. "You two smell exactly alike."

"Lilacs," said Kim.

"Is there something going on here I should know about?" Nola asked.

"Yes," said Sue and Yaz in a chorus.

"Well hurray! It's about damn time! And I've got news, too. You three deserve to know, me and Windsong were awake most of the afternoon, thinking about what you said, Sue. We can't seem to take care of ourselves or each other without you or Kim around to lean on." Kim and Sue exchanged startled looks as Nola continued. "So we did it. Windsong has decided to go to law school, and we made our phone call to Alcoholics Anonymous."

"Well!" said Sue. "In this case I'm glad you've decided to

dump me!"

"Not entirely," Nola promised with her big smile.

Yaz was right there with a conversation stopper. "I would offer to buy a round of margaritas to celebrate, but I think it would be counterproductive!"

Nola poured four more straight oranges, and they all set about to cool off. It was one of those hot nights when the Santana wind comes howling down the valleys from the desert. A couple of drinks didn't cool Kim at all. Suddenly she was gone, rushed outside for new air. Thinking about the days events, she didn't pay attention to the unfamiliar Detroit sedan as it rolled quietly into the alley until it stopped beside her.

The driver opened a window and asked, "Are you Kimmey?" His face was in shadow, his voice unfamiliar, and there was something definitely unsavory about this dude. How did they know her name? But the always sociable Kim replied, "I'm Kim." Before she could ask the question, two men were out of the car. As quick as the flash of moonlight on the chrome-steel blade, the metal slid between her ribs three times and she slumped to the ground.

Sue and Yaz had scarcely enough time to miss Kimmey when a hush came over the club, and everyone turned toward the door to see a figure crawling in from the alley. "I'm bleeding to death!" came Kim's muffled voice as she sprawled there on the floor.

Yaz, always the professional, knelt beside her, and felt around. "My god, she's sticky blood from her neck to her knees! Sue, call the ambulance! Nola, get over here with a bucket of ice and a mess of fresh bar rags!" She examined the wounds and noticed air bubbling from two of them.

After she made the call, and before Sue could consider the wisdom of passing out, Nola arrived with the ice. They wrapped ice in the rags and kept digital pressure on the three red splotches on the back of Kim's tank top.

Yaz maintained control. "Just stay there quietly, Kim. You have three stab wounds about an inch and a half wide, but the bleeding has about stopped, so it's not as bad as it could be. Say your mantra and do your transcendental meditations. The ambulance is on the way." She sounded a lot more authoritative than she felt.

Kimmey was whispering so softly she could hardly be heard. "Sue, Sue. Find Juice. Those dudes wanna get her, too. And the Ferrari is in the alley."

Sue looked all around the back and front bars but didn't find Juice until she looked on the dance floor. Juice was wandering around so high she had no idea where she was.

By the time Sue led Juice back to the bar the ambulance was there and they were loading Kim into the back. "Yaz," said Sue, "I can't leave Juice here all alone in this state—"

"But I can't do this alone."

"Of course, honey. You help the paramedics with Kim. I'll take Juice in the hearse and follow behind."

At the emergency hospital the doctor shook his head in despair. "Three deep knife wounds! That's more than I can handle here with no help. We'll have to transport her down town to County USC Hospital. Sorry, ladies."

The meat-wagon parade was on the road again. As they rolled down the freeway Kim became comfortable and sleepy, and had settled into lower and lower breathing before Yaz recognized what was going on. "Wake up and talk to me, you big jerk! You're not getting out of life this easily!"

"But Yaz, it's so peaceful. And I saw the white light at the end of the tunnel. Never be afraid of dying, Yaz. I saw—" On and on she talked all the way into the Emergency entrance at County USC.

"What will we do with Juice?" Yaz asked. "She'll catch cold in the hearse, once the heater is turned off."

"Don't worry," Sue said. "I'll bring her in here and stash her in a chair in the lobby. No one will bother her, and she won't care where she is for another four hours." Before they knew it they were standing at the foot of a gurney rolling past triage directly toward the emergency operating room. They watched the residents and attendants install pipes and machines at most of Kim's orifices, natural and artificial, and knew what terror was all about.

As they rolled Kim down the halls, the surgeon kept a running summary of her condition. "She has been done by professionals, but they were either very clumsy or had a lot of bad luck. The blow to the carotid missed, but got her upper left lung. They aimed for her heart but got the lower right lung. We're going to fix the liver after one of the lungs drains."

Sixty minutes later Kim was in the ward, awake and even talking, if slowly. "There I was, just a minute ago, just out of the O.R. and in the recovery room, all but dead. Wouldn't you know it, there were the narcs with the nerve to grill me about dope! Nevermind I was about dead All they cared about was what was I 'on'?!—Who was my 'pusher?!'—what 'turf' were we fighting over?! You'd think they would at least know the language after all these years. Some people think dope is at the bottom of everything."

"Well?" Sue was laughing, pleased that Kim's mind and mouth were connected again.

Kim smiled her knowing smile and wiggled. "Well, dope is sometimes involved along the line, but it's seldom the reason for anything. And then there's love...."

"The original Doctor Feelgood?"

"Everyone's entitled to feel good," said Kim.

"Sounds like a Constitutional amendment, to me."

The surgeon didn't let her talk anymore, but explained Kim's prognosis. "Both lungs have stopped bleeding. We'll stitch up the liver in a couple of hours, and that's all we can do for her. The main thing is she's a strong girl and has plenty of people who care about her. Right now Kim should rest up for more surgery, and you have time to eat or sleep or something else healthy."

"Why don't you go home and get a couple of hours of sleep, Sue," said Yaz. "I'll telephone Kim's dad in Santa Barbara—"

Sue nodded in agreement. "I forgot all about him. She needs him here, and he deserves to know."

"I can doze in the waiting room next to Juice until you can get back to relieve me."

"Juice! How is Juice doing?"

"It's like you said. Hasn't moved a muscle."

Outside, it was Sunday morning already. On the way to Rialto street Sue stopped by Highland House. In her stocking feet she tippie-toed upstairs to tell Danny where her people were

174

and what happened.

Danny was too sleepy to speak. She only nodded and squeezed Sue's hand giving her the kind of look that made her think maybe she ought to be told what Danny was thinking. Danny hugged Silver and went back to sleep, revealing nothing. Sue went on home to a dish of hot oatmeal and a turn in her own sheets which still smelled sweetly of Yazmina. When she awoke it was nearly ten. In a flurry she drove back downtown. Both Juice and Yaz were awake and talking with a handsome, worried grey-haired man, Kim's father from Santa Barbara. "I'm really pleased that Kim has such good friends. You have all taken such good care of her, I hardly know how to thank you."

"Maybe," Sue postulated, "if we had been a little more clever we might have avoided this entire episode."

"Kim was awake the last time I was in there," Yaz said. "She wants to talk to you about something or other."

Sue was back in Kim's ward in time to watch them disconnect the pipes and help her sit up in bed. "I can't believe this!" said Sue.

"Maybe not as good as new, but the doctors here are the best in the world." Kimmey smiled her usual tough grin. "If you gotta get stuck, make sure you're in L.A. County."

"So how are you feeling?"

"Well enough to do some heavy thinking. What if we had connected for junk last night, like I wanted to? If I had been high when I was stuck, I wouldn't have had the sense to crawl back into the bar. I would have bled to death in that stinking alley!"

Sue nodded soberly. "That's probably true. Eventually I would have missed you,and gone to look for you, but would you still have been alive?"

"Obviously all you guys, the Great Beyond and my mantra have been watching out for the old Kim. Now I've got to take over. It's time I started to pay the rent and put vegetable beef soup on the table."

Kim looked quickly out of the corners of her eyes, as if there was something world-shaking she had declined to mention. Not wanting to disturb that important thought, Sue poured Kim a fresh glass of ice water and pulled her chair in a little closer.

"Now," she said, "what I want to know is, who dunnit?"

"Who stabbed me?" Kim took a long pull on the straw in the glass of ice water. "Can you think of anyone who has something against me, someone who wants to get even?"

"N-no." Sue ruminated a moment. "Possibly Evelyn, but I don't think she has this sort of thing in her. Patty? She's jealous, of course, but I think she would rather see you degraded than dead. I've got no answers for you."

"I've had plenty of time to think about it, that is, between grillings from the police. Anyhow...I had never seen the guys who knifed me before, but there was something familiar about them. I think I recognize their style. Patty's connection in Hollywood! Not the man himself, but a couple of his cronies."

Sue frowned quizzically. "What have they got against you?"

"Nothing." Kim contemplated a while. "but they do have a grudge against Patty."

"So spit it out already!"

"Well, a few months ago Patty got busted for carrying grass. She never said so specifically, but I got the idea she got off by rolling over on that dealer."

"You mean she gave evidence against him?"

"Yeah," replied Kim a bit impatiently. "Rolled over on him. I think they were getting even by doing me, as if I was an appendage of Patty, like the Ferrari. If you want to make somebody hurt you hurt the one they love."

Sue nodded gravely. "The stabbing does seem to connect to Patty and the slashed tires on the Ferrari."

Kim nodded slowly and whispered, "For sure, for sure. How little they know how little she cares. She might even cheer. Lie down with dogs, get up with the mange."

"I hope you kept all this from the cops and the media. Otherwise they'll find you again and you're dead meat!"

"Whoa, Sue! You've been watching too much television. When he gave the order for my head, it was probably a spur of the moment thing. He was most likely high and paranoid. Heroin makes you paranoid sometimes. By now he has enjoyed the report of my demise in the alley. He has probably forgotten I ever existed."

"Just the same, I'm going to get Karen and Danny down here, and one of us is going to be here with you all the time until you get out. Only the nurses and doctors are getting into this ward!"

"I really appreciate that, but it won't be necessary," Kim said with a sly smile. "I'm getting out, off to a place he will never go." On that cue there was a rustle behind the white curtain. Flor stepped out, as bright as the Virgin of Guadalupe.

"You're all packed," said Flor to Kim.

"We're eloping to my grandmother's ranch in Wyoming," said Kim, as puffed up as her bandages permitted. "After the cops left this morning, I got to thinking, not a usual thing for the old Kim. I just about 'bought the farm' last night. Think about it. If I had died right then, I would have spent my entire life without Flor! I figured I owed us a real chance to be happy. So I telephoned her at Highland House, and she said *yes*, and here we are! We'll rest up in Big Sur a few weeks, and then stop off at Stinson to ship my shit and pick up Narcissus and Goldman. We're going to leave the Ferrari in Salt Lake City for Patty's finance company to find."

Sue gasped at the audaciousness of the scheme. "How are you going to get the black Ferrari?"

Flor was smiling and chuckling softly. "It's out in the parking lot. After you left Highland House this morning, Danny sneaked into the garden shack and woke me up. When she told me the whole story, I knew exactly what I should do. Furthermore, she had Kim's car keys."

Sue chimed into the laughter. "Now Evelyn *and* Patty will be out after us all!" When Kim was safely strapped into the passenger seat of the Ferrari, Sue did a word or two of thanks to Qetzalcoatl and the Great Beyond, finishing off with a run through Kim's mantra. It's a long trip to Wyoming.

"Danny knows where we've gone, but don't tell anyone else, please," said Flor. "Come and see us next spring when the fish are running."

"I promise," said Sue, just before she began crying. "You can't beat 'simply wonderful'!"

Flor let out the clutch slowly, mindful of the dozens of Kim's stitches, internal and external. As the Ferrari eased into the street, Kim reach into the glove compartment, pulled out a cassette and shoved it into the slot. The car came back and as it made a slow, tight circle around the friends staying behind, Kim turned up the sound.

As the music and the Ferrari disappeared into the slow, quiet, late Sunday traffic, Sue felt two warm arms around her middle, and two hands in the front pockets of her cut-offs. Yazmina whispered into her ear, "Let's go home and lock ourselves in your studio again."

"That's what I like," Sue replied, "a take-charge woman."

Epilogue

For old time's sake Sue parked her new Chinook mini-motorhome by the park. As she locked the cab door behind her, a squadron of eleven wild geese taxied down the street and over the bridge on surveillance. When they had acknowledged the new arrival they adjusted their flaps and slipped into the brackish water of Linnie Canal.

Feeling duly welcomed Sue tucked her hands into her pockets and strolled down the Linnie quay toward Highland House. Something underfoot went soft and squished as she stepped over the picket fence into the yard. In the flower garden beside the gate, this year's crop of plastic dolls' hands and faces were a sure sign that Danny Mae still lived there.

She knocked at the door. The door swung open and there stood Danny, blonde and brown. "Sue! Welcome home!" Danny hugged her solidly, and then held her at arm's length. "You can come in, but you gotta leave those sneakers outside."

Sue looked fondly at her bright-whites, and then looked questioningly at Danny. "But Danny, they're brand new!"

"You've been gone so long you can't even walk and stay out of the dog-shit!"

"How soon we forget." Sue kicked off her shoes, revealing virgin athletic socks.

"Would you look at those! Brand new, I'm betting."

Sue wiggled her toes in the comfort of unmended cotton. "I'm still apprehensive of relative opulence."

"The last we heard from you, you got that job at the Jet Propulsion Lab," said Danny.

"I'm still there, working on the Voyager ground program, processing the data and pictures from outer space."

"I'm surprised you're back into technology again."

"Are you a Ray Bradbury fan? He says there's nothing but technology, that everything we do involves getting a living out of the earth. What I can't do any more of is make killing machines. I got so I couldn't stand that jerk I used to be."

"You paid your dues long enough. Just remember, you can always move back to town and get your mind organized again, if you ever need it. Now for the important stuff. How about you and Yazmina?"

"She's got a nice job at the new Sleep Studies Center at the Huntington Hospital in Pasadena. How did I get so lucky, getting a woman like Yaz?"

"I always knew you'd find someone who could manage you."

"You had more faith in me than I did. You'll have to admit I was a champion loser."

"A loser? I'm sorry, Sue, I just can't see you as a loser. We all needed you, in our own ways. I hope you got something out of it, that's all."

Sue had to laugh. "Of course I did! I learned how to hang out and I learned a trade, as opposed to a profession. I discovered my own mystical powers. I learned how good it feels to wear new socks and...."

"But forgot how to keep the bottoms of your shoes clean! So what brings you back to the ole' plantation?" asked Danny. "It's been quite a while."

"It's feeling like summer, and you know all lesbians get mushy. So I got mushy."

"Well all right! Wanna see the pictures?"

Sue went inside with Danny. "You mean you have pictures of all that stuff? I can't believe it."

"I was busy all the time with my Instamatic. Kim and Little Karen gave me some of their pictures." She set herself on the couch and twisted around just enough to reach a thick, spiral-bound album which just fit on the coffee table. "And here we have it, yards and yards of gorgeous lesbians, all in color...our Kodachrome days." They opened the album and began.

Danny Mae sighed softly as she ran her fingers across the

pages of pictures. "It's been at least a year since any of the old gang came to town."

"In a way I'm glad to hear it," Sue said. "It means everyone is doing well. How is Charles doing?"

"Well, the restaurant merged with the bar, and Charles and Elsie have two amazing children, blonde and black at the same time, and so smart they frighten me."

"So the war is finally over for Charles."

"For all of us." said Danny. "And Nixon is gone." But Danny was brooding. "There was so much evil, I couldn't stand it, couldn't do anything about it."

"We did try to make life more pleasant and healthful for those in our immediate vicinity."

Danny nodded. "Gradually the Establishment got its shit together, and everybody split. You wouldn't believe it. They all have jobs, businesses, houses, cars and credit cards. There are even horses and boats. I hear Nola has a house on the sand in Malibu"

"I see Nola and Sapho and Thea in the movie credits, where they all belong."

"Talk about your high dramatics, Windsong passed the bar, and is Public Defender."

"Perfect! At last, she has brought guerrilla theater indoors! What happened to Karen?"

"Well, the last time she was in town Nola took her to join Alcoholics Anonymous. I got a letter from Michigan, and another from Oregon."

Sue nodded her approval. "She finally answered the call of the open road. I felt she was uncomfortable in that miracle apartment with all the furniture. She kept giving her space away."

Danny began giggling and finished with guffahs. "I think you've uncovered something!"

"What about Katherine and Cherry and the kids?"

"Well," answered Danny through a sly smile, Katherine wasn't getting any help from Cherry, so the kids are in still Marin with their dad. Cherry is a topless dancer in Seattle."

"At her age?"

"I hear she has a loyal following."

"Do you hear from Kimmey?"

"Let's see. Kim and Flor have made a good thing out of the fly-fishing ranch, a semi-vegetarian dude ranch."

"So," said Sue. "Kim finally answered the eternal question 'Who's going to take care of Kim?' I was afraid she had turned extended adolescence into a life-style! Speaking of kids, tell me about Juice."

"Juice was always a sturdy personality. All she needed was the time and space and love to grow up in. She finally graduated from Cal State Northridge and lives in the Valley, making buckets of money working for some big developer."

Sue laughed. "I can't imagine that bunch, all cleaned up and reformed!"

"Reformed is a bit too strong a word. Actually, we still like to hang out and turn on, after work."

"Everyone is entitled to feel good, as Kimmey would say. Life, liberty and the pursuit of happiness...."

"Whatever," said Danny. "If you're missing one, you miss them all. We at least kept everyone alive and high and mostly out of jail..."

"...with a couple of notable exceptions. When you come to think of it, much of what we did had something to do with keeping someone alive, or trying to keep moving, at least."

"Hmm," mused Danny. "Our one big failure I'm afraid to report. It's Evelyn."

"Well, come on," begged Sue. "What about Evelyn?"

"For one thing, she shot herself in the foot. Prophetic, eh what? Then she had a child, badly narcotics-damaged."

For once in her life Danny was almost sad. "Evelyn is one of my closest friends, but I was never able to do anything about her."

"Don't be so quick to judge yourself, Danny. We were all a bit crazy, but Evelyn was so afraid of the world and had such a rotten self image. That's hard to change."

"The only one I know who has really changed is Patty, and we had nothing to do with that."

"Patty? Changed?" said the surprised Sue. "The Great

182

Beyond moves in mysterious ways."

"Patty was and still is a sharp number. She's into real estate. For eight years she has been with the same woman, a rock singer, and lives in Torrance, 'Where The Sewer Meets The Sea.'"

"And you...whatever happened to Danny Mae?"

"Remember that red-head I met at the Bacchanal? We were together for five years, and next month I'm going down to Mexico to visit with her and her husband and two babies."

"And you said you were never cut out for motherhood!"

Then Danny said philosophically. "I've been trying to figure out what it is that makes Venice so enigmatic to outsiders."

After a short contemplation Sue said, "Envy. Simple envy."

"But we were so poor, hungry so often, hopeless. True, we had good times, but is that enough to envy us?"

"Not quite. We learned how far we could fall before we pick ourselves up. They don't know that about themselves yet, so they envy us."

Danny crossed one foot over the other and slipped into her poetic mode. "We were like an island in the river that disappears when the drought is over."

Not to be out-done, Sue crossed her feet. "When Lafayette returned to France after the American Revolution was over, he took with him enough American soil to cover him when he died. I feel the same way about the Venice sand."

"Far fuckin' out! We're high again!"

The beer was all gone and evening had come to Linnie Canal by the time Danny had turned the last page of bright Kodachromes. She and Sue sat there quietly, listening to the last echos of their old friends' laughter and whispers slipping back between the covers of the album as Danny put it back in its place on the shelf, ready for the next Highland House alumna to open it.

THE LIVING END

Fritzie Rogers was born in Sioux falls, South Dakota in 1927, and graduated from South Dakota State College. She worked in the areospace industry as a computer programming engineer, and was a graduate student at UCLA in Anthropology. She now lives in Sierra Madre,California.

Other Books from New Victoria

Mysteries by Sarah Dreher

A Captive In Time—Stoner finds herself inexplicably transported to a small town in the Colorado Territory, time 1871. When, if ever, will she find a phone to call home? ISBN 0-934678-22-7 ($9.95)

Stoner McTavish—The first Stoner mystery—Dream lover Gwen, in danger in the Grand Tetons. *"Sensitive, funny and unabashedly sweet, Stoner McTavish is worth the read."* ($7.95) ISBN 0-934678-06-5

Something Shady—Stoner gets trapped in the clutches of the evil Dr. Millicent Tunes. *"The piece de resistance of the season...I think it's the funniest book I ever read."* ISBN 0-934688-07-3($8.95)

Gray Magic—Stoner and Gwen head to Arizona, but a peaceful vacation turns frightening when Stoner becomes a combatant in the struggle between the Hopi Spirits of good and evil. ($8.95) ISBN-0-934678-11-1

Mystery

She Died Twice — Lauren—The remains of a child are unearthed and Emma is forced to relive the weeks leading up to Natalie's death as she searches for the murderer. ISBN 0-9-34678-34-0 ($8.95)

Woman with Red Hair—Brunel—The mystery of her mother's death takes Magalie and her French lover Danielle, into the slums of France, her only clue the memory of a woman with red hair. ISBN 0-934678-30-8 ($8.95)

Death by the Riverside—Redmann—Detective Mickey Knight finds herself slugging through thugs and slogging through swamps to expose a dangerous drug ring. ISBN 0-934678-27-8 ($8.95)

Romance/Adventure

Touch of Music— Clarke—Roxanna and Becky are part of a lesbian household. Conflict plagues their relationship until Roxanna's daughter is hospitalized, and they find that their differences are not so important. ($8.95) ISBN 0-934678-31-6

Kite Maker—Van Auken—A tough dyke who's never had a girlfriend drives up to a women's bar in a spiffy new Cadillac convertible...and drives off with Sal on a wild adventure in search of a long lost friend. ($8.95) ISBN 0-9346768-32-4

Cody Angel—Whitfield—Dana looks for self-esteem and love through emotional entanglements—with her boss, with Frankie, a bike dyke, and Jerri, who enjoys sex as power. ISBN 0-934678-28-6 ($8.95)

In Unlikely Places—Beguin—Following a dream of exploring Africa, nineteenth century adventurer Lily Bascombe finds herself searching for the elusive Miss Margery Pool. ISBN 0-934578- 25-1 ($8.95)

Mari —Hilderley—The story of the evolving relationship between Mari, an Argentinian political activist, and Judith, a New York City musician. ISBN-0-934678- 23-5 ($8.95)

Dark Horse—Lucas—Fed up with corruption in politics, lesbian Sidney Garrett runs for mayor and gets more than she bargained for when she falls in love with a socialite campaign worker. ISBN-0-934678--21-9 ($8.95)

As The Road Curves—Dean—Ramsey, with a reputation for never having to sleep alone, takes a break from a prestigious lesbian magazine to go off on an adventure of a lifetime. ISBN 0-934678-17-0 ($8.95)

All Out—Alguire—Winning at the Olympics is all-consuming goal until romance threatens Kay's ability to go all out for the gold. ISBN-0-934678-16-2 ($8.95)

All Out—Alguire—Winning at the Olympics is all-consuming goal until romance threatens Kay's ability to go all out for the gold. ISBN-0-934678-16-2 ($8.95)

Look Under the Hawthorn—Frye—Stonedyke Edie Cafferty from Vermont searches for her long lost daughter and meets Anabelle, a jazz pianist looking for her birth mother. ISBN-0-934678-12-X ($7.95)

Runway at Eland Springs—Béguin—Flying supplies into the African bush, Anna gets into conflict with a game hunter, and finds love and support with Jilu, the woman at Eland Springs. ISBN-0-934678-10-3 ($7.95)

Speculative Fiction

Cathy IV - Lucas- Explores issues as well as being a fun adventure and love story. Jenny falls in love with a woman who may not even be human. ISBN 0-934678-41-3 ($8.95)

Shadows of Aggar—Wolfe—Amazon, Diana, born into a woman-only society is an undercover agent on a medieval planet. There she and Shadow guide, Elana attempt to prevent all-out intergalactic war. ($9.95) ISBN 0-934678-36-7

Promise of the Rose Stone—McKay—Mountain warrior Issa is banished to the women's compound in the living satellite where she and her lover Cleothe plan an escape with a newborn baby. ISBN-0-934678-09-X ($7.95)

Humor

Cut Outs & Cut Ups—A Fun'n Games Book for Lesbians—Dean, Wells and Curran—Games, puzzles, astrology, paper dolls. ISBN-0-934678-20-0 ($8.95)

Coming Out— More Fun'n Games —Dean, Wells and Curran-- puzzles, humor, advice for Lesbians ($8.95) ISBN 0-934678-33-2

Found Goddesses: Asphalta to Viscera—Grey & Penelope—"*Found Goddesses is wonderful. I've had more fun reading it than any book in the last two years.*"—Joanna Russ. ($7.95) ISBN-0-934678-18-9

Morgan Calabresé; The Movie—N. Dunlap—Wonderfully funny comic strips. Politics, relationships, and softball as seen through the eyes of Morgan Calabresé. ($5.95) ISBN-0-934678-14-6

Short Fiction/Plays

Secrets—Newman—The surfaces and secrets, the joys and sensuality and the conflicts of lesbian relationships are brought to life in these stories. ISBN 0-934678-24-3 ($8.95)

Lesbian Stages—"*Sarah Dreher's plays are good yarns firmly centered in a Lesbian perspective with specific, complex, often contradictory (just like real people) characters.*" — Kate McDermott ($ 9.95) ISBN 0-934678-15-4

The Names of the Moons of Mars—Schwartz—In these stories the author writes humorously as well as poignantly about our lives as women and as lesbians. ($8.95) ISBN-0-934678-19-7   Audiotape read by author ($9.95) ISBN 0-934678-26-X

Women's History

Radical Feminists of Heterodoxy—Judith Schwarz—Revised edition. Original research about a club for unothodox women that flourished in Greenwich village from 1912 through the thirties with many fascinating photographs from the era. ISBN 0-934678-08-1 ($8.95)

Available from your favorite bookstore, or order directly from
New Victoria Publishers, PO Box 27 Norwich, Vt. 05055